Goose River Anthology, 2010

Edited by

Deborah J. Benner

Goose River Press
Waldoboro, Maine

Library of Congress Card Number: 2010907693

ISBN: 978-1-59713-099-8

First Printing, 2010

Cover photos by Kasey Benner

Published by
Goose River Press
3400 Friendship Road
Waldoboro ME 04572
gooseriverpress@roadrunner.com
www.gooseriverpress.com

Table of Contents

Table of Contents

Table of Contents

Table of Contents

In Memory of

Marguerite Sylvester

Kathleen Czarnecki
Kenilworth, NJ

The Devil, the Dragon, the Day After....9/11

The day after
smoke from the dragon
boiled through its nostrils
Smoke from the dragon
sent by the devil
held a smoldering, plastic noxious stench

So quiet the streets
no cars speeding
no sirens screaming
our people were speechless
The day after

No planes swimming through flocks of clouds
Just choppers hanging overhead
to protect us from he who freed the dragon
His breath blew black
the ash of man

*First published in *Tales from the Boulevard,* **Goose River Press**

Sharon Lask Munson
Eugene, OR

Composition

The garage door opens.
You turn off the engine
it sputters and stops.
I slide out of the passenger seat
legs rubbery after too long in the van.

Grabbing bags from the back seat
I enter the house. You follow,
arms full of travel treasures—
glass bowls the color of sand
watercolor, blue pond with goldfish.

I toss maps and books on the rocker
walk to the windowsill
where one African violet
wilts in the dim.
The silence distracts me.

You walk into the living room
give the pendulum on the old wall clock
a poke, and the heart of the house
begins again, measuring
the sweep and drift of our lives.

Nina M. Scott
Amherst, MA

Remembering Marguerite

As a long-time summer resident of Friendship, I have ever been bothered by the abyss between many townspeople and the summer folk. It's not wholly a question of being outsiders, as some of the summer families have been there as long or longer than some of the villagers. Some of it may come from the fact that the summers are short, and seasonal residents are focused primarily on family and other visitors, as well as recreation, while the townspeople, rightly or not, may perceive the summer folks as wealthier than themselves. The way the town is constructed, with summer houses on points of land and the village inland, may also be a factor. In any case, the chasm exists.

As I am an admirer and sometime disciple of Don Quixote, a few years ago I decided to set out to right what seemed an obvious wrong. I am also a believer in the power of food to bring people together. If I could convince people in both camps to give me family recipes, ones that were embedded within family stories, I would then create a community cookbook which would accomplish several things: get people to know more about each other; share family stories (some of which might involve people from both communities); and get some good recipes. Once this was done, I envisioned a shared feast at the town community center which would break down the barriers once and for all. Sounded doable.

I began my quest by talking to people in the town who had a lot of contact with the summer folks—"bridge people" I called them—and every one told me exactly the same thing: "You've got to talk to Marguerite Sylvester. She just finished doing a cookbook with the Friendship-Cushing Seniors, and she'll give you good advice." Marguerite had been a long-time elementary teacher and later principal of the Friendship Village School. Herself a summer person from Mass-

Nina M. Scott
Amherst, MA

achusetts, she had married local lobsterman Charlie Sylvester and knew the town and its ways well. "Even though I've lived here since 1938," she later told me, "I'm still 'from away.' That's all right. That's just the way it is."

I called her and she invited me into her home. Marguerite was then eighty-seven, a small woman with white hair and bright blue eyes which looked at you and the world directly. She had some Parkinson's and difficulties in walking, but her mind was sharp as a tack and her sense of humor well-developed. The first thing she said was, "Doing a cookbook is a lot of work." As work didn't daunt me, I set out to talk to both townspeople and summer people, telling them why I was doing this project and why their cooperation was important to me.

For two years I tried to pry recipes and family stories out of people—with no response at all from either camp. I was crushed. Marguerite was not surprised. "That's just how folks are," she remarked. Meanwhile she and I had become close, and through her I had gotten to know many others in Friendship who have also become friends. The cookbook project might have failed, but my own bridges were under construction, especially to her.

We shared a love of books and of writing. She owned a computer and used it actively, also for e-mail. Marguerite and her daughter Linda went regularly to a class of memoir writing, and she would show me pieces that she had written. She wanted very much to be published. Her chance came during Friendship's bicentennial (2007), in the creation of *Friendship Homes. If These Houses Could Talk*, a book which concentrated on the history of the town through its structures. In this venture both town residents and summer folks collaborated, and Marguerite was by far the most prolific contributor. Not only did her own memory go back farther than most, but she was a fierce researcher. Friendship's history was very important to her. In our many conversations about this project she made it clear how much she admired

Nina M. Scott
Amherst, MA

the capacity for sheer hard work and endurance shown by men and women who had lived there in earlier times.

I was also struck by her frequent and unselfconscious references to God in her life. Her Bible always lay at her side, full of tags and notations. Initially Marguerite was not a faithful Christian, but Charlie had been, and had shown her the way. There is a story about Charlie's faith that is still remembered in Friendship today: he was out lobstering and had forgotten to bring his lunch. He got hungrier and hungrier and finally began to pray. Shortly afterwards a still-sealed TV dinner came floating by on a board. "Did you eat it?" he was asked. "Didn't dare not to," Charlie answered.

In our conversational ramblings, we sometimes touched on politics and on the economic crisis. Washington politicians, in her opinion, engaged in "a fearful amount of pushin' and haulin'," most of it to little effect. When the economy really soured, Marguerite went straight to the crux of the matter. "People make a little money and then they get all foolish and decide they've got to have a bigger house and cars they can't afford. Spending money you don't have is a bad idea. I have to have my furnace fixed before winter and I'll have to do without to get that paid for. Right now I owe $19.76 on my credit card and that's how it's going to be. Maybe I should go to Washington and show them how it's done." I thought it was a great idea.

Local lobsterman Greg Havener, who had had Marguerite as an elementary school teacher and knew her for many years, was not surprised at her stance. "She was an in-charge kind of person," he said of her, and she would agree with that assessment. In a piece of memoir writing she referred to herself as "the dictator," as when she galvanized her reluctant seniors to engage in a Christmas cookie swap. "You really shouldn't let me get my foot within the door, for I will no doubt take over," she wrote. Once on a roll, she gathered their recipes, typed them up on her computer, printed and bound them, and organized the swap in conjunction

Nina M. Scott
Amherst, MA

with a luncheon for her often lonely and housebound peers. All unclaimed cookies were gathered and distributed to shut-ins and members who could not attend. "It beats sitting around and being bored," she said in a letter which accompanied my own copy of the recipe booklet.

Marguerite often engaged in written dialogues between "Body and Brain"—her increasingly frail body hampering her still very active brain. Though I fought it all the way, this past summer I could see that she really was failing. In September Linda confided that she had contracted leukemia and that the end was near. Summer was over and I had to leave, knowing I would probably not see her again. Two weeks before she died she wrote me a letter: "Body is confined to a hospital bed and not particularly content. Brain is still in high gear." Was it ever. During a phone call I told her that I was teaching a graduate seminar. She pounced. "Do they have it on the Internet? Do they let seniors audit the course? What text is involved? Would there be a charge? Can you guess my train of thought?"

Marguerite died on October 21, 2009. In charge to the end, her last project was to have one hundred Christmas stockings made, filled and sent to soldiers in Maine's 286th Army Combat Battalion, stationed in Afghanistan. She died before they were completed, but other women in Friendship saw to it that her last effort was realized. Because of publicity as to her project, there was a $450 surplus in donations, out of which phone cards for the soldiers were purchased.

In our last conversation she was calm about being near death. "God has been very good to me. I'm ready. It's fine. All is well."

Sally Belenardo
Branford, CT

Leading a Double Life

A tree without a leafy crown
looks like a tree turned upside down,
bare branch and twig the counterparts
to root and rootlet underground.

Its trunk divides the tree in halves,
one hidden and one seen.
The part we know grows green,
takes a path toward sun, turns
summer light to sugar,
yields the fruit of all its labor,
holds a breeze close, whispering,

while its invisible other reaches
for nutrients and water found in soil,
an anchorite, blind and earthbound—
free, however, from weather's wrath.

***

Starlings

From winter branches
dark leaves drop, fly up again.
Listen: The trees sing.

Carol Leavitt Altieri
Madison, CT

Lord of the Arctic

In frigid Churchill Bay,
eerie twilight of polar night,
I have come to watch the huge
and sleek white bears
dozing in the shadows of sculpted
icebergs. Over the shifting surface
of packed ice, dead spirits
bathe the landscape sending
messages of aurora borealis.

Wind whips the hollow, transparent
fur that keeps bears warm
in watertight suits. Over the crest,
a tireless swimmer wakes,
hoists himself from ice floe
thunders away for miles
over the frozen wilderness. Snow
geese flap wings on retreating ice.
Other bears on the horizon
are seen to be in a mirage.

Sniffing out the breathing holes
of seals, taking the day by storm
the polar bear rears up,
flings itself through smoking sea,
heaves huge weight down, crushes
a harp seal's head with a single blow.

Carol Leavitt Altieri
Madison, CT

Lying in ambush, an Inuit throws
a harpoon—anchors the bear's body.
Polar bear sweats with fear
as he tries to struggle free.
In a savage conflict, other hunters
cry, mimicking their raven companions.
Inuits kill Nanook,
legendary white bear
needing its power to travel deep
in the seas or high to the moon.

Despite Summits, worry hangs
like a storm of erupting
solar flares across every Inuit home.
Our illuminated brains won't save them
in the end. The Arctic swarms with ghosts.

***

Sally Belenardo
Branford, CT

The Pet Canary

Calling a mate he never found,
the captive bird would sing,
voicing the longing in his heart,
perched on a metal swing.

Only his song escaped the cage,
where he remained enclosed.
Only his silence set him free,
on flightless wings reposed.

John L. Campbell
Brookfield, WI

Hand-Me-Downs

Dead men's clothes haunt my closet,
Dick's sport coat, Paul's slacks,
and Grant's sweaters, Art's high
winter boots hang in the garage.
Widows never give me anything,
they offer to my wife, a go-between,
with words like, *Maybe this will fit.*

I often wear a blue whachamacallit,
a pullover with half-zipper front,
once worn by my friend, Grant.
He didn't give it to me,
his widow gave it to my wife,
and my wife said, *Try this on,*
and I asked, *Where'd you get this,*
and she said, *It was Grant's*—nice
fit, so I wear it while walking,
which makes me think of Grant,
so the pullover has some positive
life-after-death affects, except
my thoughts revert to his death.

The day he died, I crept out, left
his room, unable to watch him
shake, tossing in bed, out of it,
trying his best to die with dignity,
me, angry, cursing sotto voce,
asking if God was on holiday,
and our wives chatted on and on,
as though we were just visiting.

Bill Tucker
Aurora, OH

Mama in the Huddle

One thing you can say about Coach is that he's fair. I mean he doesn't hold a grudge. I thought for sure after what I said before we played Greenville I never would see the inside of the gym again, much less dress out for last night's game. It's probably because Coach is so religious and, after he thought about it, saw I was telling him the truth. That is, I really thought we didn't have a prayer but it didn't mean I was going to lay down on him in the game. I really wanted to play. He must have realized that, because he told me to come on back out Monday afternoon for practice. Another thing is we got beat thirty-nine to six, and we only scored after Greenville had pretty nearly cleaned off its bench.

And Coach never said another word about it either. Right off I started back in running signals with the first string, and Tuesday I quarterbacked a scrimmage using Clarksdale plays. That's who we played last night, Clarksdale.

He seemed kind of embarrassed about the whole thing all week and didn't have much to say to me except when somebody else was around. Of course, he talked a lot about what to expect from Clarksdale and explained how we should handle this guy Graham who could really run the wide stuff. All in all I think he realized that we could have had Red Grange and it wouldn't have made any difference against Greenville.

Before the game I was just fooling around with the other guys like I always do, getting more and more excited. But just then Coach came over and slapped me on the shoulder, not hard but in a kind of friendly way, and said, "Let's get the ankles taped, Red."

I think I knew right then that I was going to start.

Boy, I really liked Coach about that time. A fellow who can forget about somebody saying what I did and not even mention it is really okay.

Bill Tucker
Aurora, OH

All the time he was working on my ankles I kept thinking about him one way or another. In a lot of ways Coach is a funny kind of guy. He's short and kind of heavy and smiles a lot. He can be plenty serious when he has to, but he's good natured. One thing he doesn't know much about is how to dress when he gets outside the gym. On the street, I mean. For instance, when he leads the choir in the Baptist church he wears this funny get-up of a green double-breasted suit coat and a pair of light blue pants. It's the only green coat like that I ever saw. I don't belong to the Baptist church, so I don't see him every Sunday. But I go there every once in a while just for a change, or maybe when Margie wants me to. One day I saw him come in in his green and blue outfit and he had on white sneakers. I thought maybe he had just forgot he had them on, but Sonny said he wears them pretty often. You can see what I mean when I say he's a funny guy.

"Okay, Coach," I said and he must have been able to tell how grateful I was by the way I jumped right up on the bench and stuck my foot out before he'd even gone to get the tape. He smiled and cracked me across the back and went for the tape.

"That all right?" he asked and gouged me in the thigh with his thumb, testing for the charley horse I had before the Greenville game.

"Oh yeah, Coach. I never felt it at all the whole week."

We had a good talk while he taped my ankles. He just pumped me up like he always did and never a word about the fiasco of last week. He never exactly said so, and that's another reason I knew I was going to start. You never really know until he calls your name right before the kickoff. That way I guess it keeps you guessing a little. But you can usually tell by the way things have gone during the week and how he acts in the dressing room before the game. He shifts the line a little from game to game and Ralph and Lootie have alternated at right half, but most of us know we're going to start. Last week was the first time in two years I hadn't started. But I knew this time because he asked me to go over a few things about our offense that he just wouldn't have bothered with unless I was starting quarterback.

Before the game he got everybody together like he always does and gave us a little rah-rah. Not enough to be sickening like some coaches do, but just enough so you can hardly wait until the game starts. He did mention that it was his birthday.

"You fellows know what I want for a present, don't you?" he asked and grinned all around at us.

"Yea!" We all set up a big roar.

"Okay. Let's get out on the field then," he said.

We poured out of the gym running and jumping and whacking each other on the shoulder pads.

When that cold air outside hits you right after you've been in the gym where it's pretty steamy, it really makes you feel good. With nothing on but a jersey and a skivvy shirt to cover your chest, it gets right to you, and you really feel like running. And seeing the lights on, you get the feeling of the crowd before you ever get across the street to the stadium. There's something about a night game that you don't get in the daytime. Another thing that always gave me a funny kind of good feeling was walking up the sidewalk and across the asphalt street with cleats on. With your ankles taped and a thick pair of wool socks on, your legs feel different, stronger I guess. There's just something about the sound and the feel of those cleats on something hard like concrete that's hard to explain.

When we got inside the fence, the cheerleaders met us and we started to run onto the field with them leading the way. Margie is a cheerleader, and she always looks around until she sees me—she tells by my number, which is fifty four—and we run a little way, before we actually get on the field, holding hands. The cheerleaders jump and holler in front of us until we pass the bench. We go on down to the end of the field to warm up, but they stop and work up a cou-

Bill Tucker
Aurora, OH

ple of good yells from the crowd.

Fifteen minutes is all we warm up, but some teams just about run themselves to death before the game even starts. Coach says he's seen these teams that warm up for thirty minutes so pooped at the kickoff they can hardly make it down under the ball. So all we do is limber up for a couple of minutes and then start running through some real simple signals. After that, the ends run out for a few passes, and the linemen get down under a few punts, and we're ready.

I mentioned before about Coach being a religious guy so we always get in a huddle and he prays, right before the officials come over to the bench and ask for captains. He never prays that we will win, but the way he puts it about knowing we are going to play a good clean game he sort of implies that if anything dirty is done, it will be the other team that does it, God would have a hard time explaining why we lost, if we did.

Well, I said all along I knew I was going to start and Coach called Lootie and me out as co-captains. We walked out and met the Clarksdale captains and shook hands all around. The referee flipped a quarter to see who would receive. We lost the flip and had to kickoff. But we got to choose the goal, so we chose the north goal. There was a strong north wind and we could make yardage on any punting we had to do.

I've said before that the only thing more exciting than being down in the dressing room getting ready for the game is standing all strung out on the field ready for the kickoff. While you're waiting for the official to give the signal for the kick, a couple of guys in the band start this long roll on the snare drums and keep it up until the ball is in the air. I guess they can't stand to be fooling with the drums after that, because they stop and just watch. The crowd is all up on its feet and it's the first time they've been anything like quiet since we came out of the gym. It doesn't *feel* like they're quiet, though. Boy, if they were quiet *like that* all the

Bill Tucker
Aurora, OH

time, you couldn't stand it. It's more exciting than when they're screaming their heads off. Like every one of them had his eyes on *you*, and you can almost *feel* them saying, "Come on, Red. Come on, Red." It makes your face burn and it takes all the strength you've got just to stand there.

When old Fred finally does get his foot into the ball, and takes off down the field only about half conscious, you always wonder if you're going to have enough energy to even get across the fifty-yard line. It seems like you've burned up all that good strong feeling you had in your legs just standing up there waiting.

I guess you wake up when the first guy tries to throw a block into you. I think that first play takes more out of you than the whole first quarter. You're always so tired and winded after the kickoff play that you stand around blowing like an old plow horse. It takes a couple of plays before you can settle down and just concentrate on playing ball. After that you're okay. It doesn't even bother you too much on the other kickoffs. It's just that first one.

Even kicking into the wind, Fred got a long high one almost to the ten. This little guy playing left half got his hands on the ball but fumbled around with it enough for Sonny and our two ends to close in on him. Boy, old Sonny almost cut him in two.

I'm not going to go over every play. Clarksdale had about the same kind of team we had. They weren't too heavy but played tricky, fast ball. We run from the modified punt and work a lot of alternate plays that can really get to a clumsy team. We have a play, number eighty-eight, that's a quarterback spinner where I fake off to the right half and fullback and then take out around right end with the guards who have pulled out for interference. That play was really driving them crazy. I must have made six or seven first downs with it before they finally got their end to quit charging. At the end of the first quarter I let Lootie have it instead of keeping it myself and he went twenty-six yards for a score.

Bill Tucker
Aurora, OH

Right after that things started happening to me. I was playing line backer on defense, and the first play from scrimmage after the kickoff their left end check-blocked in the line and came into the secondary to take me out. Most of the time I can handle a blocker in open field by giving a little ground and using my hands. But this guy was plenty tall and he decided at the last minute on a rolling cross-body block. Boy, he wrapped all around me. When we went down his elbow got me in the nose and I couldn't see for a minute it hurt so much. When I went off the field to let Coach look at my nose, my mother was standing about ten yards in back of the bench with this worried look. Must have looked like something scary with blood all over the front of my jersey; we were wearing white again. I waved to her in a way that showed I was all right. The way I did it also showed that I wished she would go on back up in the stands.

Clarksdale scored about the middle of the second quarter. This guy Graham went wide for eighteen yards. It was my side but I didn't even see it. That big end had me on the ground again. Boy, he sure had my number there for a while. I was having so much trouble breathing I couldn't pay as much attention as I should. Coach made me wear a rubber nose guard in case I had fractured my nose, and I kept bleeding into the thing. Our manager ran up and down the sidelines with a towel and every few plays I would go over and wipe my face off and clean up the nose guard a little.

Since Clarksdale didn't make their extra point we led seven-six at the half. Coach took us onto the practice field in back of the high school bleachers and got down to business telling what we should have done and what we better do in the next half if we wanted to come close to winning. Since I was responsible for the worst play of the whole night, he got through with that first. The way Clarksdale set up their score was my fault. In the second quarter we had tried a couple of plays and they hadn't done a thing. On third down I noticed their whole secondary, even the safety, was playing

Bill Tucker
Aurora, OH

up close, about fifteen yards from the line of scrimmage. That gave me the idea of a quick kick. I figured we might get fifty yards out of it and we could rest a while on defense. It's a lot easier to play defense when you're tired. Anyway I called the quick kick. I didn't have enough time, or didn't get back far enough, or something. I was rushed so hard, I had to get it away fast, and it was a bad one. It went almost straight up and the wind caught it. I forgot we had changed goals. Besides not going more than about five yards the ball took a bad bounce and we wound up losing five yards on the play. Two plays later Graham scored and I was on the ground when he did it. Boy, Coach really let me have it.

After that he went over the stuff about it being his birthday and never expecting the whole team to let him down. We all felt pretty rotten and really meant it when we yelled "Yea" when he asked if we were going back out and show we knew how to play football. I think maybe some of the fellows were afraid Coach would get mad and substitute like he had against Greenville. Every time Coach's brother would send in a substitute so would Coach. Everybody on the bench played that night and we got beat thirty-nine to six. Coach's brother was trying to take it easy on him I guess, but Coach wouldn't let him. That's the worst a Ridgefield team ever got beat since I can remember. Anyway, everybody yelled "Yea" whether they meant it or not.

Nothing much happened all during the third quarter. We received to start the half and made good yardage the first series of downs we had. After that, neither team got anywhere near the goal line. Right at the beginning of the fourth quarter we had the ball and I called eighty-three. On that play I spin and fake to the tailback and fullback and then spin again and go off tackle. It's a check-off on eighty-eight. The left half mousetraps their left guard and, man, did Ralph ever mousetrap that guy. I never had a lineman touch me and went thirty-two yards for the score.

When we passed the bench I saw old Coach smiling and

Bill Tucker
Aurora, OH

getting all the other guys up to give us a big hand as we went by. For some reason, I went over right then and asked him if I could kick off. I knew Fred didn't mind, and I never had, and I really wanted to just once. Coach was in such a good humor he said okay.

The kick wasn't a bad one, high but pretty short. Graham caught it on a dead run at the twenty and I was down under the ball at about the thirty when he caught it. I guess after I hit him half our line piled on. I don't remember.

I think the worst thing about being knocked out is not knowing how long it's been, or what you've been doing, or what you're doing right then, when you first wake up. That's whether you've been knocked out where you're lying out on the ground or whether you're still walking around and don't know you're unconscious. Believe me, it can be either way.

This time, though, I was lying down, and the funny thing is I didn't know it. I thought I was running and I had old Graham over my shoulder. That was for just a minute and I think I really came to right after that, because I kept trying to get up. Maybe it was just that I thought I *ought* to get up. Coach was looking down in my face, and I kept thinking he probably wasn't liking the idea of me lying down out there like that.

One thing I do that Coach doesn't like so much is lie down and rest between plays when I'm playing defense. I just flop out on my back and rest while the ends trot back to the huddle, and they're fooling around getting ready for the next play. Coach doesn't like my doing that. He says it looks bad to the crowd, like I'm not in shape. But he found out I had a lot more left in me for the last quarter if I did, so he doesn't say much about it any more.

Anyway, Coach was right down in my face looking at me, and it was him that kept pushing me back when I tried to get up. He looked so worried that I figured I must be hurt, and that made me start to worry a little. I tried moving my arms and legs and they worked okay and I didn't hurt anywhere in particular. I decided I wasn't hurt and started to tell Coach I was okay. But just then *she* said, "Why don't you get Doctor Freeman? Can't you see he's practically bleeding to death?"

There she was, right there in the huddle with all the guys who were standing around and gawking like I was about on the way to the cemetery. Boy, I just couldn't believe it. But I could see her right there by Coach down on her knees looking at me.

"Aw, Moma!" I said. I really tried to get up then. She pounded Coach on the shoulder.

"Don't let him get up, Coach. My goodness! Don't let him get up," she said and reached over and pushed me back down herself.

Man, I thought she must have gone crazy. I really started to get embarrassed then. All these guys were standing around and I guess you know how you'd feel if your mother was out in the middle of a football field carrying on like that.

I said to myself, *Boy, if she's going to act like this, I wish she would stay home.* You didn't see my dad out there getting everybody all excited and embarrassing everybody. He was standing over by the bench hollering for Dr. Freeman.

Now that I think about it I can see why she got excited after she got out there. I must have looked like a corpse. In the first place there was all this blood from my nose and then I spit out a mouthful of stuff when I first tried to sit up. I didn't even know it, but what caused it was a broken vein in my throat. I've got these five cleat marks on the side of my neck. So I can see why that would get her pretty upset. All I'm saying is that she shouldn't have been out there in the first place.

Since she is making me stay in bed today, I've been going back over everything that happened and what comes back to me most is what Dad said about the way she came down out of the stands. He said when she saw all the numbers up

Bill Tucker
Aurora, OH

walking around but good old fifty-four, she figured it must be me laid out down there on the field. She waited a good long while just standing there looking and not saying anything. But when the loud speaker asked for Dr. Freeman she started down the stands taking the steps two at a time. He couldn't stop her; he couldn't even catch her. There's a waist high wire fence around the field, and he said she pulled up her skirt and took it without even breaking her stride. He said she went over that fence like a gazelle. Boy, I can see old Moma taking that fence. If she can do that in high heels she ought to be on our track team running the hurdles.

Everybody in the neighborhood has been over to see these five cleat marks on my neck. For some reason they all want to feel them, and I have to twist my neck around so they can get to the ones up under my jaw.

Every time a different one comes in Moma says, "That's all the football that boy's ever going to play." Then she comes in with them and tells them how I've lost a couple of quarts of blood and to look how pale I am.

Maybe I can get Dad to work on her, if this vein in my throat ever stops bleeding. Anyway, if I get to play next week, I hope I can persuade her not to come to the game. We'd all be better off if she'd just stay at home.

Liz Moser
Baltimore, MD & Phippsburg, ME

The Huntress

I hunt memory—
seek familiar paths and weed familiar beds;
listen for old messages in wind in wave and birdsong,
let myself be mesmerized by sound of water falling

search for who I was and how
I filled my days so effortlessly;
try through using ear, eye, touch
to reconnect, to leave
the dark and tangled thicket where I live today—

I am elsewhere
trying to recapture
substance and sustenance.

***

Why

Why am I dragged to reconnect
with that part of my life that's gone.
Why did I have to find the corner alcove in the treatment
center,
touch the couch you lay in,
be again where every afternoon
I sat by you and watched your stented arm
receiving poison—Gemzar—to destroy the stronger
poison in your fading body—did I think I'd gain relief,
a visit from your ghosted self still lying there,
instead of in the grave, in that blue suit
under growing grass.

Jean Lawrence
Waldoboro, ME

A Gray Sunday Morning

Today, before church, on this gray Sunday morning,
I stopped by the store to pick up the paper.
I was scurrying out the door when a voice caught my
attention.
"Hello, Mrs. Lawrence."

Your Peter, all grown—a man, husband and father—
Shared with me his news of the past several years.
I stood there in wonder.
What a gracious and charming adult he's become!
When I inquired of you and Carol,
He told me you were waiting just outside in the car.

I wrestled with the wind, crossed the expanse of the lot,
And my eyes caught the movement of your hand in a wave.
You rolled down your window, and we shared welcomed
greetings.
The years moved by quickly while we talked of old times.

I asked about Carol and you about David.
We chuckled over grandkids, growing old, and memories.
Of your battle you shared, "I've been fighting with cancer,
But I'm almost through treatment."
Your words, frankly spoken, tumbled on,
"But today I'm out riding in my shiny new car."

Jean Lawrence
Waldoboro, ME

"How time flies!" we said together,
And I noted our kids are now the ages we were when we
met.
"God's been good," we asserted.
"We've been blessed," we agreed.
I saw in your eyes that old twinkle of joy
Which comes of a strong faith and years of true love.

Time was up; you were tired,
And the choir was expecting me,
So we clasped hands in friendship
And said our good-byes.

You waved once again when my car turned the corner,
And I thought to myself,
"Good-bye, my brave, Christian friend!"

***

In Your Arms and Off the Ground

"August 13, 1960"
On that date, we said, "I do."
Naiveté complemented my white gown.
We were so in love with love and each other.
Vows completed, the pastor said,
"You may kiss the bride."
In haste to seal our promises and make me your own,
You surrounded me with a bear hug embrace.
My veil caught in your arms; my cap tipped.
You swept me off my feet!
Your love and exuberance for life
Have kept me off the ground
For fifty years!

Genie Dailey
Jefferson, ME

Standing at Seaside

Chuckling and stuttering,
they tumble about me as I stand shin-deep in cold water
letting little waves lap my feet.
The shimmering salty liquid numbs the skin
and washes the sand out from under me
while the little stones giggle.
As the water whispers backward toward the sea,
I feel it's me that's moving—
the stones and sand are standing in my place,
and I'm water-skiing without a boat.
Without a thought, my arms reach out for the towline;
trying to keep my ballast, my balance
until my chilly heels come to rest a little deeper
in the shore. But here's another wave!
And the tumbling, chuckling, giggling stones
resume their chatter.

Janet Morgan
Wiscasset, ME

Foggy Morning Run

Maine winters were sweet for a child of the 1950's. There was always so much to do, especially on crisp and sunny winter days, even in rural Wiscasset. On this particular Sunday morning, the rest of the family had slept in, but I got up early, for I had a mission. This would be my time alone. The sun was barely up; the house was peaceful and quiet.

Christmas was over, but I had another whole week of school vacation yet to explore. I had given much thought about the gift of these days and I had planned out each and every one.

On this day I was going down back to the stream that flowed through the property behind our farmhouse. So far my cousins, who lived down the road, had concentrated on the larger pond a mile away—the place where all the kids in town converged to skate. Today might be my last chance. I wanted to be the one to put the first marks on our stream.

I jumped out of bed and looked out the window as I began pulling on clothes. It had snowed overnight, I observed. Because my kid brother Eddie had a room next to mine, I quietly dressed in layers for warmth. I didn't hear him stir.

I slipped downstairs on stockinged feet and tiptoed towards the closet where our winter gear was stored. As I struggled into my ski pants, I recalled my discovery of two days ago. The pants were a bit small for my eleven-year-old frame. My parka still fit, as did my boots from last Christmas. One thing was new: This year's Christmas present had been beautiful white figure skates. I reminded myself that I should ask for new ski pants next year.

I bunched up my scarf, hat, and mittens in one hand as I slung my new ice skates over my shoulder with the other hand. Their extra long shoelaces made a nice handle when tied in a bow.

Janet Morgan
Wiscasset, ME

I silently opened the front door. There was no need to lock behind me, for no one locked their doors in rural Maine. I wondered if we even had a key as I slipped outside and let the storm door close on silent springs.

I was ready for action. I trod past the house, requisite outer building, and the empty space that once held a barn. The barn had blown down during Hurricane Carol two years earlier. Winter birds chirped nearby as I wadded through a few inches of powdery new snow, dragging my feet on purpose so as to leave two continuous lines in my wake. I suppose I was rubbing it in—like leaving bread crumbs so everyone would know where I had gone. As I walked, I hoped that a heavier snow would soon replace this light stuff so my cousins and I could make snowmen and snow forts together before school vacation was over.

As I got closer, I noticed a foggy mist rising from my destination. I reached the edge of the stream and plopped myself down onto a soft bed of snow. I savored the moment as I pulled off my boots and slid on my new skates.

I had dreamed of this often: how I would skate this long smooth run all by myself. This might not be a huge pond where one could skate in large circles and execute fancy moves, but the stream ran on and on and on. If I could just stay on my feet, I would sail down that stream as though I were an Olympic speed skater.

Even as I thought about it, I knew I was being optimistic, very optimistic. But that didn't stop me from envisioning my grace of movement as I flew down the seemingly never-ending stream. In my daydreams, I raced the half-mile distance, never stopping until the finish-line ribbon was breached and victory was mine. At the end of that run my cousins would be watching and cheering me on.

In actuality even if I had been a graceful skater—and I was not—I was bound to fetch up on obstacles in no time. The truth is that this stream was not only skinny, but it was also shallow. During the wettest season of the year, I could-

Janet Morgan
Wiscasset, ME

n't wade higher than my knees because that is the deepest it ever got.

Grass always grew there, breaking the water's surface. During the winter months it was still there, waiting to wrap itself around my skate runners. Dead blades always stood, proudly waving and daring skaters to pass without tumbling. I lost the bet every time. It was still a glorious experience, however, even when I picked myself up, rubbed my sore knees, and started over.

It may have been selfish of me, but I wanted that first run to be all mine. The fog settled around my ankles until I couldn't see my feet, much less the impediments that would soon signal my downfall. I pushed off anyways—and fell with a resounding crash onto the hard ice.

Ever the optimist, I saw the good side of my fall: no one was there on the sidelines to laugh at me. Once my brother and my cousins ventured down here, my skating in isolation would be a thing of the past. They would arrive with skates and sleds and muck up the ice. But for now it was all mine. And when they finally arrived, I knew what they would find: the crisscrossing of one lone skater's marks proclaiming, "I was here first."

Erik Richardson
Milwaukee, WI

borrowed light

the farmer in the photograph
rides on a solitary summer day
forever, in August maybe
on the rolling Missouri plain

tractor tracks in field grass
mark the mower's circuit of days
sympathetic shadow lines
carved in the silvery green

glowing under black-winged clouds
like ravens
a late summer rain's coming in
carried by a rusted red tractor

across the shifting slopes
the past is dragged forward
in a low, pa-dumping gear
coughing and lurching

toward the barn against the wind
eye blinks, shutter clicks
black feathers turn to stone
suspended waiting for gravity's call

but with the next breath rocks will turn
again to smoke and rain
will gradually bleed the colors away
to make way for the fall

Erik Richardson
Milwaukee, WI

into grace and winter
staring at a farmer now
in his dusty hall a part of me
will stay behind, like stone

in summer Missouri fields

*First published in *Arbor Vitae,* vol. 1, issue 2, **Desperado Press**

***

Sally Belenardo
Branford, CT

Dead of Winter

Snow, swept by brumal wind,
swirls off the roof
and 'round the chimney curls
in clouds of frigid smoke
that billow from a gable,
smothering the shrubbery below.

Night, creeping close, devours
scraps of light. Turn your back
to window by the table. Enjoy
the evening meal. Try not
to think of animals wild and stray,
what they might find to eat
or where they'll stay.

Scott J. Brooks
Omro, WI

Rowing on the Lake

I float on the calm water
into the sunrise of lemon-slate clouds.
When I talk to myself
the branches on shore softly sway.
The shaken leaves are a ritual of ecstasy,
a dervish dance.
Some of them on the surface
are merely reflections.
I focus on the mudra of rowing
then count my breaths as I pull the oars,
but my mind keeps running away.
After each stroke there are gyrating funnels,
painted puzzles
of tan and apricot, cocoa and orange.
Sometimes it seems easy
to be overwhelmed by this vivid world
as we lose ourselves in the vast forests
of the forever changing here and now
watching the humble mockingbird
and listening while
a hidden halo of light
seems to be circling above while he sings
as if we could actually see it there
whirling beyond our senses.

Philip W. Pendleton
Camden, ME & Melrose, MA

The Sweet Smell of...

It was a warm Saturday afternoon, and Jeff was relaxing on the back porch with his family when suddenly the bombshell struck. Floating on a gentle breeze was a sweetish smell. Jeff almost dropped his bottle of Budweiser. *Who can be smoking pot in this stodgy neighborhood?* His thoughts began racing. *What if the kids notice it and begin asking questions? What can I tell them? What if they recognize what it is? How can I get out of this situation?*

He looked over at his wife Mary who was blissfully reading the latest book recommended by Oprah. *She'll know what it is. In college we smoked an occasional joint. What if the kids ask if we've ever smoked marijuana? How much do they know about drugs? Or how much scuttlebutt do they get from their friends? Danny is 12, and they must talk about all kinds of things. Jennifer is only 10.* His mind went into a tailspin as he thought about either of the kids asking pointed questions, an art they had perfected quite some time ago. To make matters worse Jeff and Mary had always put emphasis on being truthful with their children and asked for the same in return. *There must be some situations where it's okay to tell a lie? Even the Supreme Court justices can give dissenting opinions. Oh mother of God, what am I saying? The Supreme Court has nothing to do with this. I've got to talk with Mary. She always knows how to handle tough situations. Isn't that what a mother is for?*

Just at that point, Mary put her book down, raised her head and sniffed the air. A look of horror mixed with panic came over her face, as though she had just stumbled over a corpse. When she looked at Jeff she saw instantly that he was apprised of the situation and didn't have the foggiest notion of what to do. She gave a nod of her head and rose quickly to exit the porch. Her brain, too, was on overdrive.

Philip W. Pendleton
Camden, ME & Melrose, MA

Maybe they won't notice. Of course they will notice. What will we tell them? Why didn't we buy a house in the country with no neighbors within sniffing distance?

When Jeff stood up quickly to follow her, Danny piped up, "Where are you guys going? And why do your faces look so funny?"

Before they had a chance to answer, Jennifer sniffed the air and said, "I smell something funny. Kinda like a sweet perfume."

Danny, the sophisticate, jeered, "Hey dumbo, don't you know what pot smells like?"

The parents bolted from the porch, nearly tripping over their golden retriever on the way. When Danny and Jennifer rose to follow them, Jeff yelled in a tone that could be heard all over the neighborhood, "Stay where you are. Your mother and I have things to discuss." At the same time he prayed, "Dear God, if I'm ever going to have a heart attack, please let it be right now!"

Mary's thinking was more realistic. "I guess we're just going to have to give them the drug talk right now. I thought we could wait a year or two longer."

"But what if it bombs the way the sex talk did last year?" replied Jeff. "Remember, Danny said he wasn't going to do all that nasty stuff, and that if he wanted kids, he'd adopt them."

"Yes," added Mary. "And Jennifer said this made her more sure than ever that she was going to be a nun." Mary didn't share the memory she was now having of her mother trying to persuade her to become a nun. *Right now,* Mary thought to herself, *I wish I had followed her advice.*

Before Jeff and Mary had time to collect their bewildered thoughts, Danny shouted from the porch, "Dad, the Good Humor Man is here. Can I have some money, please?"

"Yyyyes," stammered Jeff. "Here's a five spot, and keep the change. And Jennifer, here's five for you, too."

"Thanks, Dad," they both chimed.

Philip W. Pendleton
Camden, ME & Melrose, MA

As Jennifer went down the porch steps she paused, then turned to her father. "The Good Humor Man is smoking a funny looking cigarette, and I smell that sweetish smell even stronger."

Danny, with great scorn, "Didn't I tell you that was pot!" Now it's Danny's turn to pause. He turned and looked his father straight in the eye. "Dad, did you ever...."

Jeff barks at him, "Go get your ice cream, and don't bother me with questions."

Danny, in an injured tone, "You don't have to snap at me like that. I just wanted to know if you were ever a Good Humor Man."

"I'm sorry, son" was Jeff's reply with utmost relief. "I've had a lot on my mind today."

As Jeff watched Danny and Jennifer buying their ice cream, he raised his eyes to the sky and mouthed silently, "Oh, thank you dear God. And don't forget to cancel my request for a heart attack!"

***

Steve Troyanovich
Florence, NJ

driving such lonely thoughts

waiting for you to call
i read some Patchen poems
filling in the emptiness
waiting for the rain...
you did not call
but you are so lovely
and i am...still here...
waiting for the snow

C. H. Schnepf
New Haven, CT

Aunt Bea

Every family, I believe, has a "wise one"—
a Shaman who can stand back from day to day family
events, conflicts—and speak from love and wisdom.
My aunt was one of those "old souls."

I dreamt of you last night
How many years has it been
Since last we spoke and laughed
and discussed all those discussions
my upcoming graduation
the War which waited for me like
a cat—I the bird nervously
sitting in the sights
You listened and spoke of family
and honor and what it would do
to my father if I just said
"up yours" to the draft
We spoke of many things
of family and of Life and
discussed all those discussions
which I had no answers to

I dreamt of you last night
How thirty years have vanished
Since last we spoke and laughed
and discussed all those discussions
and then suddenly you had to
leave and I placed a yellow
rose between your folded hands
and spoke some words of sorrow
which only we could hear

C. H. Schnepf
New Haven, CT

I dreamt of you last night
I saw you in my room
and we did talk of many things
and laugh and cry together
of War which only the old
remember now of my father and of Life
Dear God how many years has thirty
years been
since last we saw each other
and I placed the yellow rose upon
your chest and whispered in your ear.

I dreamt of you last night.

***

Emily Rand Breitner
West Boothbay Harbor, ME

Epicenter: Pakistan

Most of the girls didn't run
for the exits, clattering
and shoving past each other when
the school walls began to moan and ripple—
that's what the boys did,
making it out alive to watch
their school collapse,
its corrugated red roof wrenched
and tossed like some oversized, crinkled lid
into the wrecked walls—
no, the girls ran to each other
and huddled, holding
each other,
and died.

Dawn Edwards
Melrose, MA

No Answers?

The streets look the same but where am I?
Do I go left or do I go right?
Will I know who I am when I die?
Will you be there when I waken at night?

When you look at me who do you see?
A pretty girl, a worried mother?
Where is this place I've come to be?
Am I your sister or your brother?

Faces come by and ask, "How are you?"
How am I? Who are you? Who am I?
Those thoughts I have you say are untrue?
My babe doesn't need a lullaby?

Doctor, can families get this disease?
And if that's so, how to prevent it?
We'd like it to go away, this disease
So far no research is definite.

Gemma Tamas
Surrey, British Columbia

Out of Order

It started with a stomachache, right after breakfast. Agnes stomach heaved, emptied, until only bitter bile came up. Her grandmother washed her face and put her back in bed. There, she curled up holding onto her side.

It was after World War II and Europe still lay in shambles when in all this chaos a Religious Order started. Young women, most with shining diplomas, gathered to live on a farm where they toiled the fields for their living. Only their prayers and singing disturbed the silence. Agnes' grandmother lived in the nunnery, helping the Sisters prepare their meager meals from what the land provided and looked after Agnes, not ten years old yet. The child's mother couldn't raise her, no time for her. In her profession, a young girl was a burden, an unwanted appendage. In the mornings, Agnes was taught by the Sisters, in the afternoons she was left to her own design.

Her mother wanted her to stay in the convent, to become a nun, but her grandmother knew better. She helplessly watched Agnes yearning for her mother's love, struggling to please her, while at night she dreamt about the outside world.

"Poor little lamb! What are your choices?" Grandmother lamented.

All day Agnes stayed in bed. She couldn't eat and what little water she drank, came back with violence.

"You will be alright by tomorrow," Grandmother, wiping the cold sweat from Agnes' forehead, promised her.

During the night, high fever racked Agnes' body. When morning came, Grandmother decided to take her to town.

The Sisters got the rickety wagon out, putting blankets on its floor, hitching two horses in front. Large rocks spotted the dirt road to town, causing agony to Agnes as the

Gemma Tamas
Surrey, British Columbia

wagon bumped along. Curled in a fetal position, she lost consciousness.

In town, the Sisters of the hospital carried her inside. "Dr. Raba is out of town till this evening," one of them told the grandmother. Wringing her fingers with worry, she stayed by Agnes' side. "She is getting worse by the minute," she said, stifling her cry in her handkerchief.

"I know, but we can't do more for her," the Sister calmly replied, then silently glided towards the door and closed it behind her.

"I'll pray for her," Grandmother sighed, staring at the empty wall that had only a cross above the bed. She reached into her pocket for her rosary, and as nervous fingers ground the beads on her lap, lips moved without a sound.

Evening arrived with Dr. Raba. He took one look at Agnes and ordered the Sisters to get the operating room ready.

"Don't worry, my dear," Grandmother squeezed Agnes' hand, who was drifting in and out of consciousness. "I'll call your mother. She will be here soon." Her hands were feverishly holding onto her rosary.

When Agnes was out of sight, Grandmother hurried to look for the phone. She called the nightclub where her daughter entertained her numerous male friends.

"Daughter, you better come to the hospital. Agnes is very sick." The phone stayed silent.

"She is in the operating room." Still the phone was mute.

"If you have any decency left in you, you better hurry here!" Grandmother raised her voice.

It was late at night when Agnes was back in her room. She opened her eyes and saw her mother sitting by her bedside, clothed in an evening gown, her painted face more annoyed than worried.

"Don't move, darling. Everything will be all right." The mother leaned forward, fleetingly kissed Agnes on her forehead. "Don't move! There are tubes coming out from your

Gemma Tamas
Surrey, British Columbia

stomach to drain away the bad things from your inside."

"I'm thirsty," Agnes moaned, stirring on her bed.

"You can't have anything to drink yet," her mother smiled with relief. "It is a good sign she is thirsty," she said as she furtively glanced at Grandmother, who's face was appalled to see her ready to leave.

Grandmother stayed all night, helplessly watched Agnes' stomach expanding, feeling the child's pain as her own. She sat there, staring into empty space, questioning why an innocent life had to suffer so. "Let me take her place," she begged, but nobody was there to hear her plea.

Come morning, Agnes was back in the operating room. She didn't wake up for days, her life dangled on a frayed line ready to snap.

On the fifth day, she opened her eyes. Her fever had subsided. She looked peaceful but said she felt like her whole inside had been ripped out. Grandmother silently prayed by her side, knobby fingers still holding her rosary. The child's mother sat rigidly on a chair close by.

"She can't have any children," Grandmother whispered.

"She can't wear a two-piece with that scar on her stomach!" mother rebuked.

With pain-filled eyes, Agnes looked up to her mother's face, seeking her forgiveness, but she, defiantly turned her head away.

Agnes closed her eyes. Her grandmother leaned forward grabbing her hands, trying to pull her back. But it was in vain. Agnes' life silently slipped beyond the reach of her grandmother's loving hands.

Jim Mello
Farmington, ME

Snow Walk

the solo
cross country skier

as he huffed past
craggly faced

framed by hair as gray
as the snowing sky

awakens the demons
of aging

which torment the reflections
in the waters below the bridge

the teen
gliding past with her father

who glances back at her
to mark his territory

checks me out as we pass
not knowing

my daughters were scattered
like milkweed seeds years ago

or how the ghosts of failures
haunt with

each crunch of snow
along the weathered path

Jim Mello
Farmington, ME

as the two crows
slice the vacant airways

one cawing incessantly
the other lamb silent

except for the whirring of fluttered wings
propelling it

through the maze of trees
and the sound of

one woodpecker pecking,
tapping into

memories and experience,
the brushes dipped into

the inkwells of imagination
and swirled

in the colors of
sound

for the sake
of art and sanity

e. w. oestreich
Damariscotta, ME

The Old Ones

The old ones learn to sit and wait
with folded hands.
And through thin spectacles they stare
toward yesterday.

The old ones learn to wait in quiet rooms
to hear an absent voice
that went away to somewhere
else.

And mothers who, once, sang a child to
sleep with lullaby are sung, by children now
grown old,
to quiet rest.

They would return to ruined gardens
where paths no longer lead and
where no lilac fragrances an April
air . . . because they are no more.

The old ones stay enclosed within the
narrow limitations which they've set like iron bars
of old remembrances, secure—where once they
ran in open fields.

The old ones, not recalling names, keep still
a bit of Spring
before they turn and simply sit
and learn to wait.

Robert Erickson
Round Pond, ME

The Blue Lady

Squint hardened gaze on the harbor soft
To tell-tale clouds wisped by winds aloft.
Salt soaked hands, finger the worn out chart,
The tide's in his belly the breeze in his heart.

On the coast of Maine in a harbor round
North of Pemaquid on Muscongus Sound
Lies a little blue sloop ready to run,
Wind, water and wake before this day is done.

Haul the halyard and raise the main
Drop the mooring, ne'r heed wind nor rain.
She cuts water clean on wind so fair
Clearing harbor, this beauty, her man, a pair.

She beats to windward this blue hulled woman,
Heeled to the rail and up to the coamin'.
Her stays are screaming, the wind blows gale
"Give me more" she cries, "don't slacken sail."

More he gives with his tiller held high,
This blue clad lady he cannot deny.
She shudders and hums in close hauled glee,
A cry from his lips, "What more d'ya want of me?"

The voyage is over, the work is done.
He turns the lady home on a downwind run.
Her white wings spread from side to side,
She wallows and sighs so very satisfied.

Robert Erickson
Round Pond, ME

Home to Round Pond with mooring in sight
Clearing South Point rounding the marker tight.
The blue lady slips home, her purpose is through
"When do we sail?" she says, "again, I want you."

*First published in *The Poetry of a Life in Maine,* **Goose River Press.**

***

C. H. Schnepf
New Haven, CT

Easter Dinner

A smile in everyone's eye floated across
The wide table
Through the crystal wine glasses,
Bouncing off bone china dishes
Reflecting in pepper and salt shakers
Crystallized over crushed ice olive platters
Flickering captive in butane candle dance
Passed on up the cream napkin resting
On lace linen handed down from the dead,
Caressing the edge
To the eyes of the beholder
across the table smiling back.

Helen Vandepeer
Pembroke, Ontario

Agnes, 1895

Agnes swung her black button boots back and forth, higher and higher, admiring the swishing of her blue skirt. Swish, swish, not many girls had black button boots around where Agnes lived. She toyed with the idea of scraping the boots along the ground and scuffing the toes but there were too many big sisters around to tell on her and Mommy was already cross because the roast chicken had been tough. Sundays were so boring, first came church, and then the roast. Agnes was the youngest of the four girls. Maud lived in the city with her husband Jack. Prue was stepping out with the local minister, Davis; he had already spoken to Father so they would be married soon. Now Dolly had gone and found herself someone to moon and sigh over.

Agnes made the swing go even higher; it was horrid being the youngest. Dolly used to be fun to be around until she left school last year and started wearing her hair up. Now she walked around in her long skirt and white shirt with a little brooch at her neck pretending she was much older than just sixteen. She was far too much the lady to play hide-and-seek or roll-a-hoop...and now she had grown up work, helping mother, and sewing with Aunty. *Eleven is such a lonely age,* thought Agnes.

It was 1874 when Father, Uncle Hans and Aunty Mary came all the way from Denmark to make a new life in Australia. They landed in Queensland in the far North of the Continent where a terrible flood took all their possessions and nearly drowned them. They worked their way down and across until they reached Adelaide in South Australia where farm land was available.

Uncle Hans and Aunty Mary were the first to settle here and then Father married Mommy, who was born in Australia, and they followed soon after. The area was named

Helen Vandepeer
Pembroke, Ontario

after Uncle Hans who built a church and school on his land. Children were taught to read and write on weekdays and on Sundays the building was used for worship. The elders preached, but once a month the preacher rode his pony from town.

It was one of those Sundays, so Prue and Davis were on the side porch talking with Father. Agnes bet to herself that they wouldn't know Dolly was sitting behind the Acacia with that William person. She grinned as the swing slowed to a sway. Perhaps someone ought to go and see what Dolly was doing.

She jumped from the swing managing to land just short of her longest ever jump and looked with distaste at the boots. Soft slippers were the best for jumping in; boots dragged her back and you couldn't play hopscotch or run in them.

Father had worked hard to clear the land of its stunted eucalyptus trees with stumpy roots that broke the farmers plough. Mallee scrub it is called; line stone country where the rocks rose to the surface every year. The farmland was dotted with mounds of stone, all picked up and moved laboriously by hand. Its tough country with a low winter rainfall but it yields a good wheat crop and the sheep give a nice fleece of wool. There was money now at last after years of back breaking labour to pay for a hired hand, a servant girl for Mommy and a few luxuries such as the despised boots. Other little girls at school could only dream of such things. Her best friend Dulcie Brewer longed for a pair of boots like these.

Agnes pushed the long curls away from her face and tiptoed around behind where Dolly was sitting with her William, William Wood, Willy Wood; what a silly name. He and Davis were friends otherwise he wouldn't be here; they were both staying for tea of course.

Agnes heard Dolly prattling on and William's quiet earnest replies but it was difficult to make out exactly what

Helen Vandepeer
Pembroke, Ontario

they were saying. If she could just get close she might hear something to tease Dolly about. The tree they were sitting under wasn't sturdy but Agnes, slight for her age, felt that she could safely climb into the branches. *Careful now, don't make a sound.* She scrambled in a most unladylike fashion into the tree and leaned down over the budding romance.

Unfortunately the tree was weaker than Agnes expected and the branch she was lying across broke with a snap. She fell with a yelp into William's surprised lap and found herself looking upwards into twinkly blue eyes in a gentle face adorned with the loveliest auburn hair she had ever seen. It was one of the few times in her life she was lost for words.

Dolly jumped up screaming with fright half feigned, half real. She would have fainted except that William's arms were full of her wretched little sister and her new white blouse could get dirty. She bit the end right out of her silk glove instead. What was she going to tell Father and Mummy, sitting alone like that with a single man?

William carried Agnes into the house calling for help as he went, such a little bundle all scraped and her pretty skirt torn. Mummy and Father met him at the door and followed him into the parlour, Father giving instructions while Mummy wrung her hands. His bundle gently lay on the sofa William backed respectfully away and allowed the parents an anxious check. No bones were broken. Just a small cut on her arm and a graze across her cheek.

Dolly stood in the doorway ready for flight, and Prue and Davis took the opportunity of a private moment for a quick handclasp and a squeeze around her tightly corseted waist. Lips brushed against lips briefly, sweetly, before they joined the melee inside.

Order was eventually restored. The little maid brought everyone, herself included, a nice cup of tea and Mummy was persuaded not to call the doctor out. It was a fourteen mile round trip in the pony trap which reminded Davis that he and William best be getting home, otherwise the evening

Helen Vandepeer
Pembroke, Ontario

dark would find them still on the road.

Respectful goodbyes were said all round and the two young men rode off on their horses. Agnes was put to bed; Mummy was sure that she was running a slight fever. Dolly and Prue made themselves scarce; one to dream of her young man, the other to worry what her fate would be when Agnes told how she had ended in William's lap.

Agnes drifted off to sleep, a cooling cloth laid tenderly across her brow; dreaming precociously of a pair of blue eyes and strong male arms; dreams way beyond her eleven years.

William went back to the city looking for regular work worthy of a nice young man whose family had come down in the world. He wouldn't return to the district for several years. By then Dolly was married and young Agnes had grown into the pretty girl that the child has promised to become. William courted her and they were married before she turned eighteen. This I know, because they were my own dear grandparents.

Jeannie E. Roberts
Chippewa Falls, WI

New Year's Resolution

Gwen stood before the mirror
inspecting her aged physique;
TV ads forced this exam.
Between *Botox* and *Bowflex*,
she supposed bifocals wouldn't
make the youthful resolve list!
Gwen felt old-looking in glasses;
plus, her lines didn't help matters.
Plow marks plunged between her brows.
"A nice crop could grow in there!"
Gwen chuckled at her remark.
"Is fifty the new thirty?" No!
"Lying is the new honesty!"
She recalled the lying line
from a Christmas catalog.
Gwen laughed at its downright truth.
Brummell strolled up to greet her.
He licked Gwen's soft, sagging thigh.
Though fifty-six in dog years,
he was the fountain of youth!
Brummell's fur coat was ageless—
no crow's-feet, lines or wrinkles!
Gwen looked deeply into his eyes.
Brummell had all the answers.
Why hadn't she thought of that?
Gwen giggled at the concept.
Not bad; perhaps it's doable.
Why not?! She would find a way!
Gwen's New Year's resolution:
Grow a face-to-foot fur coat!

Lilli Buck
Bristol, VA

Tecumseh's Drums

The sky was constipated, with clouds that would not burst.
The heat and humidity hung upon the landscape like a
curse.
The grassy fields were turning brown; the gardens would
not grow,
And the cornstalks stood a-withering, row upon row.

Tecumseh went out to dance for rain. He shook his rain
rattle again and again.
He chanted and he danced and he beat his drum,
With a rum pum pum pum pum pum PUM,
And he danced until he heard the thunder come.

When the clouds began to roll and bump,
Tecumseh beat his drum with a driving thump.
And when the clouds began to roar,
Tecumseh beat his drums some more.

The thunder came with a smashing BOOM!
The sky went black as a sinner's tomb.
When the lightning flashed across the sky,
Tecumseh gave an eerie cry.

When the hard, hard rain started falling down,
Still Tecumseh danced around.
He shouted and leaped like a man insane,
In the storm and wind and driving rain.

"Tecumseh, Tecumseh, come inside!"
Thus called to him his loving bride.
"What if a lightning bolt should strike?"
Tecumseh never broke his stride.

Lilli Buck
Bristol, VA

"But if I should stop and come inside,
The rain will cease, the storm subside.
Then all the creek beds will run dry,
And stone will be the riverside."

Tecumseh drummed and danced and screamed,
'Til swollen were the little streams,
Until the withering corn returned to green,
And sprouted were the little beans.

And the old ones say, in the Shawnee Hills,
They can hear Tecumseh's drumming still.
When the land is dry and the wind is still,
The earth begins to throb and thrill.

When lightning strikes a tree aflame,
The fire roars out Tecumseh's name.
It speaks the Shawnees' ancient claim,
And tells Tecumseh's noble fame.

And when the rumbling thunder comes,
They say they hear Tecumseh's drums.
When the rain pelts down with a steady beat,
They hear Tecumseh's dancing feet.

It beats and beats and beats and beats,
And beats and beats and beats and beats,
Until the air is fresh and sweet,
And broken is the summer heat.

Kristen Lindquist
Camden, ME

Bald Mountain: Celebration

Lately I've been drawn to catalog the mountain's
inhabitants, its quirks, putting stories to places:
here an old hunting camp rots to the ground,
here pines hug the mountain, flagged by wind,
here a barred owl often calls, falcons migrate past each fall.
Turkey vultures have nested here for thirty years—
I remember the day I saw the first one soaring overhead.
Here, a man swears he saw a mountain lion,
and his wife tells of a cave deep enough to hide in.
From here, breathless, I watch sunset cast its glow,
and think about how I'm almost forty.

A guy I knew in high school once hiked up Bald
with a case of Bud strapped to his back.
Nothing happened to him up here—he
and some buddies partied, slept out,
came down in the morning. I just like the story,
its celebration of foolish youth and my friend's
bull-headed athleticism. I like to think of it
when I'm hiking up myself, what it would feel like
to make the climb in the dark with that weight on my back,
but also, to find my old friends waiting at the top,
seventeen again, strong and crazy as ever.

Kristen Lindquist
Camden, ME

This spring a friend spent her sixtieth birthday
perched near the overlook. A light rain fell.
Throughout the day family and friends made their way
up the path to pay homage to this graceful guru
with pond, valley, the whole green town at her feet.
So now I carry her story with me, too, as something
to look forward to in twenty years, though
I wonder who in my life will be around then,
and who will be willing to thus exert themselves
in my honor, with or without the case of Bud,
as I wait with the hawks on the mountaintop.

***

Christine Lin
Brooklyn, NY

Warrior

Bandit eyes appraise a cloudless night
Tips folded across his back
He's pausing
For the blameless sun to rise

The blooming jasmine shuts its pores
As the inkstone comes alive
Becomes a wash of indigo across the Eastern sky

Reflect it so
Upon willful heart, unblemished soul
Two wings formed to fly
One mouth pointed full of questions
A spirit to defy

Daniel Jamieson
Candler, NC

Sodium Pentothal

You cannot lie to me—
Layer after angry layer
Truths yield themselves
Exposing the nakedness
Of your deceit.

The lies are but misguided pride,
A sense of entitlement
That waxed the strings
To my disbelief
Hypnotizing me, blinding me,
Awakening forbidden passions,
Effusing them throughout
My aging body elevating
Intracranial pressure,
Sparking higher cortical
Functions with the joy
Of the finale of a Mahler
Sympathy—a mega-dose
Of brass and kettle drums;
A startling creative truth.

You prevaricator!
Make truth the keystone
Of your creative genius.

Hannah Fox Trowbridge
Harpswell, ME

Aloft

Standing barefoot on the deck of our 40 foot ketch (our year round live-aboard-in-Maine experiment), I paused, took a deep breath and then stopped. What was I thinking? Go aloft in a bowswain's chair up the mast to the top? What then? If I survived that, I was supposed to fix the stuck halyard, then get lowered down carefully to the safe, solid, slightly swaying deck. Getting winched aloft meant that I had to trust my husband, Frank, to crank on the winch enough times to haul me up there. Neither one of us had ever done that kind of thing before. Well, since I weighed 135 pounds and he weighed 235 pounds, no question about who. Me! Then again, that little hero voice inside my head was jumping up and down like a little kid saying, pick me, pick me!

So, okay, I gave in to that bratty little kid and took my second big breath before getting my bottom arranged in the little square bosun's chair, careful to not entangle legs, arms, or any other appendage I could come up with on the way aloft. Frank managed to get me all the way to the top of the mast with pauses to check on my vertigo and any other possible scared out of my wits possibilities. Once at the top and come to think of it, all the way up, I noticed with a bit of oh-my-gosh alarm, the ever increasing arc of the mast's sway back and forth from the ocean swells and the wind. It had something to do with centers, fulcrums and the like. Didn't matter! I just held on tighter!

Once at the top, that little kid that had been jumping up and down, down there on the deck, was a bit quieter, as in, this is cool, but can we crank me back down now? I told her to hush up at that point, because having made it to the top and unjammed the halyard, I wanted to take in the swaying view, my adventurous accomplishment and just stay a moment in the whole essence of being there. (Even though I

Hannah Fox Trowbridge
Harpswell, ME

can't honestly say that I loved it.)

Too, maybe there was some reminiscence going on of when I actually was that little kid who loved to climb as high as I could in my neighbor, Mrs. Coughlin's maple tree. And all the while my mother calling from across the street for me to climb right down out of that tree right now!

***

Patrick Kielty
Beaugency, France

The Cycle of Spring

Light lingers longer now in the soft, oft drizzled sky,
And birds have long ago left their winter refuge, mild
Breezes and bright blooms having lured them to fly.
I can feel the hand of spring sprung upon my thighs and
Smell it in the full scented air that fills the fields and
Valley with the whiff of early wheat and late sown rye.
Gently dusting winter webs from saddle and spoke,
My bike and I seem young again, as if we just awoke.

Newly minted spring summons, beckoning with cry and call
Of the many streets lying before me, spurring me swiftly
Along, pushing me up those first savage little hills that fall
Before the fall that comes one day when the willing wind's
No longer there, when I may no longer dare the high and
Rising road upon which my hopes have always been
pinned.
But so long as I can still pedal uphill, I can struggle and
strive,
I know that for yet one more aspiring spring, I'm still alive.

Jessica Furino
Scotch Pines, NJ

A Three Year Old's Gift to His Grandma

Matthew was three years old and as Easter approached he told me how much he missed his grandma (his grandma had passed away three months ago). Matthew and his grandma were very close. Grandma lived only two miles away and we were blessed to see her almost everyday. Esther was a wonderful cook and would always make Matthew's favorite meals; meatballs and pastina. She always had time to spend with us and she always made that time special. She was a loving, generous, intelligent and kind woman. We all miss her, immensely.

Matthew asked me if we could do something special in remembrance of her. I asked him what he thought she would like and he asked if we could do something special for the children at the "hospitable," since Grandma had always wanted to volunteer there but was never able to. (Grandma didn't drive and was so involved helping our family and friends, that she never fulfilled this wish.) We talked and Matthew suggested that we ask his classmates, in pre-school, to all go shopping and donate gifts to make Easter and Passover baskets for the children. Matthew made a flier, we collected all the items and the children made seven beautiful baskets for the children at Children's Hospital. Matthew and his friends delivered the baskets, met with some of the children at the hospital and were given a wonderful tour of the facilities. Our children learned that it is easy to transform an idea into an action that can benefit others. We learned to listen to their ideas and facilitate their charitable thoughts.

It is seven years later, and we continue to make baskets for the children. The donations are from Matthew's school, our church's Mother of Pre-schooler's group, and the families from Woodside Chapel. Last year, we made 65 baskets (it turned out to be the exact number that was needed). We dis-

Jessica Furino
Scotch Pines, NJ

tributed them to our local children's "hospitable" and Emmanuel Cancer Foundation (a local chapter that supports children and families with cancer).

Thank you, Matthew, for inspiring such a lovely gift in memory of your grandma, Esther. We love and miss her and are so grateful that her kindness, love and faith can live on. A special thank you to all of the families who have donated their time and gifts for these children.

*First published in *Tales from the Boulevard,* **Goose River Press**

***

Diane Wood
Belfast, ME

Another Hook...

Caught on another hook—it sinks painfully deep
With the tearing of flesh and letting of blood...
But who sees—at the ocean's edge it is dark—alone
With no eyes or ears—just a loud heartbeat and eternity...

Fighting to escape normalcy—don't want to be average
Need the edge, the quest, the climb—the torment...
Hunger for the revelation—the discovery of the
Unseen—to know the hidden—to touch the tribal...

Too much is lost—the seed is dead and the womb
Bore but once—the senses still scream into the night
With a maddening effort to grasp the real and to
Find the one who casts the hooks...

P. C. Moorehead
North Lake, WI

The Look of Memory

I looked at the photo in the morning paper. An old man gazed at the World War II Memorial in D. C., recalling events that had shaped his life.

I remembered my dad, a World War I vet, sitting in his frayed gold chair, the one he had brought from the family home when he moved to my sister Irene's house. A bad bout of flu had scared him out of his independence.

"Where are they?" he had asked, as he always did when I visited. "I took particular care of them. I told you girls to pack them well."

"Dad, I'm sorry. I did pack them well. I know they are important to you."

"Black Jack Pershing signed the citation."

That citation had hung on the living room wall all through my youth, the Victory Medal pinned to the bottom of its frame. I had answered, as best I could from the scanty information that Dad had provided, the questions of friends about the medal. "Yes, my dad was in the trenches. He was gassed. The medal was given to everyone who served."

"Where were they packed?" Dad asked, calling me back to Irene's living room.

"I wrapped them in muslin and put them in a box, then put the box in one of the old trunks. Irene thinks the trunk was accidentally given to the used furniture man."

"One of the trunks was given away?" He seemed incredulous.

"Apparently."

"Well, how many trunks were there?"

"No one seems to know, but there are three left, and Irene says the medals aren't in them."

He slumped lower in the chair. *How,* I wondered, *could we have given a trunk to the used furniture man?* We had agreed that the trunks were to be saved for storage and filled with family mementos and pictures. Boxes of canning jars had gone on the furniture man's truck, and rocking chairs and lamps, and an old couch, but no trunks had been loaded, I was sure of that.

So much of Dad's life is gone now, I mused. *No wonder he wants the awards back.* Dad had left his Midwest home at twenty-two to enlist in the army. Overseas, he had met Mom, and, after a three day courtship, they wed in Paris before he went to the Front. Now, here he was, fifty-some years later, a widower with two grown daughters—but no citation and no medal.

"What happened to the trunks, Dad, the ones we brought when you moved here?"

Irene walked into the room. "They're in the basement."

That night, as she and I did dishes in the kitchen, I said to Irene, "Dad seems to be frailer. I'm used to seeing him strong."

"He has a good life—grandchildren to pay him attention and hobbies that interest him. Most importantly, he can still read, and he loves to do that, but I wish he would give up on those awards. They're gone."

"Irene," I looked directly at her. "I want to check the trunks."

"I checked them years ago. They're not there."

"I shouldn't have packed the box in the trunk. I should have just taken it and held it in my lap on our final trip here. I thought of doing that right at the time, but I didn't. I've always known what those awards meant to him."

Irene, with a glare, dropped the dish towel and went to the door, in the corner of the kitchen, that led to the basement. She held the door open, and I began walking down the steps. I hadn't been in the basement since Irene and her husband, Vince, had first bought the house years before.

At the base of the stairs, a panorama of debris greeted me. Not a single space was available to step from the stairs into the room. Cartons of books, unused furniture, and strewn clothing blocked every move. In the midst of that, two trunks stood, piled one on top of the other, like a mighty flagship. At their side, like a companion convoy, stood a third trunk.

I wedged an ankle between a carton and a folding chair and waded in. Irene followed, as I pushed through the flotsam and jetsam, the detritus of years of living.

"If the top trunk is too heavy," I told her, "we'll never be able to move it to see into the bottom one." *Besides,* I pondered, *where would we put it if we could move it?* Every flat surface, including the top of the convoy trunk, was piled high with cartons, shoes, tools, auto parts, and discarded toys.

I longed for air. *There's not a place here,* I thought, *for a child to play dress-up or to run free out through the sliding door to the grassy slopes beyond. Where,* I wondered, *were the photo albums of family pictures that I had organized years before? What else was lost here in this salvage bed of living?*

"Irene," I said, "let's start with the side trunk." I scooped items from the top of it and piled them on the path we had made behind us. Seeing Irene's troubled face, I assured her, "I'll return them to their place when we're finished."

Together, we tugged on the trunk lid. "What if it's locked?" I asked. "Do you have a key?"

"There's no key," Irene replied. "There never was."

We freed the lid. A tray filled the top. We clasped its corners and tilted it on the pile behind us. *I'll put Dad's treasures here,* I had said to myself on that moving day; now, I slid my hand down along the inside of the trunk's right side.

My fingers stopped as I felt the soft give of a cardboard box. I tugged the box upward, my hopes rising at every pull. Holding the box to the light, I could see it was from Farrell's, the little shop in our hometown owned by Mom's friend, Edith Farrell. I lifted the top and unfolded the cloth; there was the tarnished medal nestled on the faded citation with its familiar black frame.

P. C. Moorehead
North Lake, WI

"Well, I'll be," Irene said. The color rose in her cheeks. "Dad will be glad."

That night, as I approached his room, I heard tapping. Through the open door, I could see Dad hammering a small nail lightly into the wall. He stood back to pick up the citation. Feeling for the wire at the back of the frame, he tilted the citation against the wall and slid it down until the wire caught the nail. Then, he stood back again to make sure the frame hung straight.

"It's perfect," I said. "Do you want help putting on the medal?"

He looked at his gnarled hands. "I guess I do."

The pin from years ago was still in the medal's ribbon. "What was this medal for again?" I asked, pushing the pin into the bottom of the black frame.

"It's the Victory Medal. Everyone who served got one."

"And this?" I pointed to a star attached to the ribbon.

"That's a Citation Star. It's for heroism. I was wounded."

"You were wounded?"

"Yes, in the arm, while saving two men."

"You saved two men under fire?"

"Yes, they were wounded. Somebody had to get them out, so I crawled out and pulled in one, then went out and got the other." He said it matter of factly.

"You were a brave man, Dad."

"I was a young man. I wonder what those fellows are doing now. Maybe they're not even alive anymore." He touched the ribbon of the Victory Medal. "I'm old now, and I'm tired. I miss your mother; I miss my friends; I miss my old home; and I miss the opportunities I never had or never took."

"Dad, I'm sorry these were lost for so long."

"I'm sorry they were lost for so long too, but now they're back. Dear, when I die, will you take these?"

I blinked my eyes. Dad had never before talked of death. "I would love them. I'll hang them in my home, Dad, by your

P. C. Moorehead
North Lake, WI

picture. I'll put a little flag in the corner of the citation. Okay?"

"Why?"

"I want to tell the children how Grandpa went out, with his flags flying."

He chuckled. "I hope that's true."

"Why don't I make us some tea, Dad? You can tell me what happened on that day so long ago, when you saved those two young men."

"It seems like yesterday," he said. "I remember it now."

***

Janice Babcock
Wauwatosa, WI

You

You are unique.
The sun shines on you.

You share your special talents.
You freely give your gifts.

You are a Good Samaritan.
We receive your random acts of kindness.

You bring joy to your family and friends.
You brighten our days.

You are in our hearts forever.
We smile when you come to mind.

Earl Weigelt
Winslow, ME

Squirrel, Meet Marten...

Taunting, agitating, twitchy
tree-borne nuisance above,
loudly castigating all mere mortals
doomed to humble
plantigrade existence
beneath.
Scolding, vociferous, meddlesome,
farcical clown;
a tiny furbearing Polonius
spouting his stocatto opinion
to the far-flung corners of the wood.
Oh, how he loves to irritate
the canine world, flirting
with disaster at root level,
astonishingly able to
swap sides and trunks in a blink!
But more potent medicine awaits,
for his ruddy nemesis,
more agile and determined than he
(and never heard from),
gives swift answer to such insolence;
happy and able to make a meal
of him in the treetops!

Mollie Schmidt
Rome, ME

Imaging

A tint of aqua merges with rose
beneath the burning golden strips of cloud—
a Chinese sunset,

and I am on the dock amazed at
beauty—and not there at all,
but in the darkest hole

in the bank under the rocks,
burrowing beneath sweet-smelling
pine needles for warmth and rest

and food for my little ones,
relying on nose and teeth for safety;
by turns digging and darting,

freezing as the pouncing,
dark-tailed fox comes near, or
white-head eagle spies my shape;

my shape on the dock
grows dim to me, the glow fading,
color going, eyes turn inward

in the dark, feeling for the shape
of me, the mother mouse or the
mouse-trapper, prey or predator.

Diane Reitz
Winter Park, FL

After a Day on the Water

Bright eyes, red faces
bracing an opposing wind.
Useful hands that shake from
effort, needed to

hoist crisp sails,
cleat lines against a brisk
blue day—the shallows avoided
the boats glide near the harbor

The sun dulls down
behind the island pine trees.
Laughter amplifies its travels
across Round Pond

Mixed with the low talk of
lobster boatmen—churning home
in the evening—after spending the
day with their own slice of ocean.

Glancing at the blue bold water
for those who stay home and
await the boats to become known
between the two peninsulas

After a day on the water,
home—a vested, sweet place
to reflect on the sun, the waters
impudent sailors, how they mastered.

Diane Reitz
Winter Park, FL

Lie about with comrades to
complement the strengths,
not mention deficiencies,
toast the day, and each other,
they burst in the door

Loud—a wave of life breaking at the door
pouring in—salty, strained,
circus voices—and full with
seaman's stories in their pockets

after a day on the water.

***

Sally Woolf-Wade
New Harbor, ME

The Old Garden Remains

Tall fierce grass tries to smother
daylilies bravely outliving
the gardening hands of a grandmother
the empty hole surviving
the old red house that sagged
windows carefully removed
ridgepoles roughly dragged
away with the patched and leaking roof
making space for a designer's mansion.
All that is left is the long sweep
of waving field, Northeast wind,
and the Atlantic Ocean,
where iris nod and Forget-me-nots weep.

Edward O. Barsalou
Kittery Point, ME

Dear Dad

If I only had one minute
To speak with you again
I'd tell you all the little things
You missed since you went away.
You're on my mind alot these days.
I see you when I dream,
And only wish I could have been
With you on that final day.
I traveled with my son.
We came from far away.
We talked of how we'd find you there,
We'd bring you hope and cheer.
But of all the things I could have said,
Of all things left undone,
I only wish I'd been on time,
For one last final hug.
So as I think this thought of you,
I know you're close to me.
Know this "DAD" I'll always love you for all eternity.

Lena M. Fleischhacker
Kalamazoo, MI

The Sock Factory

When the sock factory's whistle blows on that white-hot August morning at 10:30, Ruby Jesup runs out of the kitchen, slamming the screen door against the jamb, then races up Bonebright Street, making sure she doesn't step on any lines in the pavement. It's bad luck.

Bonebright is a steep, uphill ribbon of concrete ending with cement steps that rise to a plateau, whereon is spread UNION TOWN TEXTILES.

Every time Ruby sees that sign, she thinks that "textiles" is a ridiculous name for socks, the only thing that Union Town makes. But, maybe, she also thinks, that's what socks are called in some place far from Union Town, Georgia. Like up North, a mysterious country where it snows all the time and people talk funny. Maybe there people say, "This morning I put on my shoes and textiles." Or, maybe, imagines Ruby, who is ten years old, maybe some little Northern child says, "Mom" (not 'Mama')..." my textiles have a hole in them." And the mom replies, "Well, dear," (not 'honey')...you can't be running around with holes in your textiles. We will just have to send down to Union Town, Georgia and get you some new textiles." Ruby giggles at the thought.

Besides trying to keep her bare feet from staying on the hot pavement too long, and trying not to step on lines in the sidewalk, Ruby is racing against the grinding sound that will follow the sock factory whistle and magically open the mill gates to let first shift workers out for 10:30 dinner (not "lunch"), because "dinner" is the name for the mid-day meal in Georgia.

She stops at an imaginary halfway mark between the mill and her grandparents' rented millhouse, the last house on Bonebright. She thinks that the mill owner, Mr. Birch G. Bonebright, personally pulls the switch that makes the whis-

Lena M. Fleischhacker
Kalamazoo, MI

tle blow and opens the mill gates.

Ruby knows that there are two Mr. Bonebrights, brothers named Burl N. and Birch G., who came in 1930 from up North to Union Town, Georgia to build the sock factory. They came to hire Georgia farmers, who had lost their land, houses, livestock and everything else but the shirts on their backs and were glad to get a job for 25 cents an hour.

The brothers, an enterprising duo, also built all the rental houses on the streets beyond the front gates of the mill; and every house has a little room off of the end of the porch, so that mill workers can rent a room to a country cousin or an old maid aunt and make an extra 50 cents a day.

Inside the mill, there is even a store, called The Commissary, where mill workers can buy their groceries and purchase sock seconds and thirds cheaply.

Today, Ruby Jesup, who dreams of someday getting a job at the mill, maybe as a turner or a knitter, bounces from one bare foot to the other as she waits at a spot that she thinks is about halfway to the mill. She thinks ready, set, go and reaches into the air and jerks an imaginary chain and on the count of three, there is a grinding sound, which opens two cyclone fence gates and out comes a parade of colorful print dresses, blue denim overalls and plaid flannel shirts.

Suddenly Ruby squeals "Granddaddy," and goes crazy waving her hands at Sam Dawson, a head taller than anybody else. Walking straighter and faster than anyone, her grandfather moves ahead of the crowd, reaches into the bib pocket of his blue denim overalls for a flat, red Prince Albert can of loose tobacco. Still walking, he raises his left hand, which holds a small sheet of thin, white tissue, into which he measures the tobacco, spilling none, closes the tin and returns it to the bib pocket. With both hands, he twists each end of the thin sheet and raises the therein confined tobacco to his mouth, swipes his tongue longways across the cigarette and slips it between his lips.

Lena M. Fleischhacker
Kalamazoo, MI

Head above his fellows, his handsome gray fedora sets to the side, a poor man's crown askew. His right hand, concealing a stick match, drops to his side, slides along the leg of denim overall, ignites a tiny puff of fire that rises to the cigarette and seems to disappear magically when Sam Dawson, the rhythm of his brisk walk never changing, extinguishes the match fire with a nicotine golden thumb and forefinger and discards the match into his overall pocket.

When Sam meets Ruby halfway home, his walking stride is unchanged. He takes the cigarette from his lips and presses the smoking end between his fingers and puts the residue into his pocket. Down to the second, Sam times the making of the cigarette and the smoking of it.

But, mostly Sam Dawson's time is measured by the call of the sock factory whistle, even though he has a watch on the end of a gold chain in the bib of his blue overall. He rarely winds the watch; but he does often trace the loop of the chain.

For half a century, Sam has carried the watch, given to him by his mother, Alma, when the family got home from his father's funeral. He was eight years old; and with the gift of the watch, as the oldest of six, he was "the man of the house."

The rhythm of his walk still unbroken, Sam greets Ruby with a smile; and wordless, he takes her hand. She runs to keep up with him; they cross the dirt yard and enter by the screen door into the kitchen. Which is not his kitchen, nor is the house his, nor the dirt yard his, any more than is the time of day. None of that has been Sam Dawson's since 1929, now twenty years past, when he could not pay the final payment on his house and twenty-acre farm.

But he does not dwell on the past. Sometimes when he is sitting on the front porch of the millhouse with a neighbor who starts talk of the past, Sam says, "My past was swallowed up by the Big Hole of 1929." He speaks with loyalty of the Bonebright brothers, who in exchange for his time, gave him the means to survive and to provide for Maggie and their nine children.

Early in 1945, two of their sons went to the "front." They were proud boys, and when they came home for their last furlough, they dressed up in their army uniforms and went uptown to Bryant and Dranes Studio and posed together for an 8 x 10 sepia tone. Mr. Bryant put a little color on their cheeks, and the blue blue of their eyes he did exactly right. The boys, it seemed, had hardly walked out the door, when Maggie and Sam got two regrets to inform you, less than a month apart.

The boys still smile from their place on the mantel piece. Maggie sometimes takes the photograph down and talks to them, runs her hand over each face. Sam goes out on the front porch when Maggie takes the picture down.

Today, Maggie Dawson has prepared her husband a boiled dinner, served on a chipped, age-stained, flowered plate. His beverage of choice, this hot day in August, is a steaming cup of black, unsweetened, chicory-laced Louisianne coffee.

None of the food on Sam Dawson's table is from the mill commissary. Food, (he calls it "bread and butter"), is Sam's priority provision; and today, Friday at 3:35 when his shift ends, with check in hand, he will leave the mill through the back door and enter a tunnel beneath the railroad tracks that separate uptown from milltown. At the end of the tunnel, he will follow the tracks to uptown and the Citizens Bank.

A gentleman, as soon as Sam enters the bank, he will remove his gray fedora and go to a pretty young girl at the teller window. She will cash his $16.00 check (four dollars was withheld already by the Bonebrights for rent on the millhouse).

In eighteen years, Sam has never missed a day of work and has risen from the darkest ranks of working man's poverty, when he got 25 cents an hour in 1931, to double that in 1949. He watches his money. He will proudly deposit $2.00 into a special savings account for Maggie, which she knows nothing about. The little savings booklet, carried with his father's watch in the bib pocket of his overalls, registers $728, accumulated over seven years. Nobody knows about the wealth he has amassed, because Sam Dawson does not talk money; and this money is for Maggie, to see her through hard times if he precedes her in death.

The young girl at the window will smile as Sam counts out two quarters for his and Maggie's weekly insurance premiums: one dollar for a girl to mop the kitchen for Maggie, and another dollar for the laundry to be picked up and returned to the millhouse door. The last request will be for a liberty half dollar for Maggie because she has been saving up for a dress pictured in *The Atlanta Journal* Sunday supplement. The pretty girl will smile again when she hands Sam a tiny white, open-ended envelope for the $3.00, which he will leave on the supper table beneath the salt shaker.

And finally, Sam will put on his fedora, and give the right side of the brim two quick jerks to acknowledge the pretty young girl behind the teller window.

With the remaining $11.00 of his week's earnings, and a grocery list he wrote the night before, Sam will retrace his steps along the clay path beside the tracks, down the hill to Homer Lumpkin's grocery store. Homer will fill the order and will collect a quarter for delivery of the groceries to the millhouse back door on Saturday morning. That is tomorrow.

Now, on this Friday of rituals, August 12, 1949, Sam sits at the head of the table and removes the fedora. He pulls from his hip pocket a softbound cowboy book and reads while he eats. Besides cowboys, he likes baseball, *The Atlanta Journal* and Democrats. Sam believes that Herbert Hoover and the Republicans caused the Great Depression, which caused him to lose his house, land, livestock and everything but the shirt on his back. He believes that Franklin Delano Roosevelt and the Democrats saved the

Lena M. Fleischhacker
Kalamazoo, MI

country.

As Sam eats, while reading of cowboys, he traces the loop of chain that holds his father's watch. He knows when to put the book away and pours the hot coffee into a deep saucer. He blows upon the coffee and steam rolls up. He consumes all the coffee at once and wipes his mouth on the sleeve of his flannel shirt.

The mill whistle blows at five minutes before eleven. Dogs howl. Sam Dawson stands, pushes his chair to the table's edge, and is out the kitchen door, the flat, red Prince Albert can already open as he measures loose tobacco into the tiny thin sheet. Ruby Jesup runs along the sidewalk beside her grandfather and tries not to step on any lines in the pavement because it is bad luck. She stops at the halfway mark and watches him begin the steep climb up Bonebright Street.

At the top of the hill, Sam Dawson turns back toward Ruby Jesup and appears to look beyond her to the millhouse. His neighbors pass around him and hurry to the factory gate.

Ruby saw him reach into the bib pocket of his overalls. He brought out his father's watch and his knees buckled as he crumpled to the sidewalk like a loosely-strung puppet.

"Granddaddy," Ruby called, and ran up the hill and the gray fedora rolled toward her, then stopped, the brim down and the crown up and she kept on running and stepping on lines in the pavement.

On the plateau, Mr. Birch Bonebright pulled the switch that caused a grinding noise, then a crescendo of steel against steel. The mill gates closed and people turned and looked back to Bonebright Hill.

"Granddaddy...Granddaddy...."

Ron Moore
Fort Worth, TX

String Quartet

When I think of what I have,
and what I've let go,
the coloring and texture of
all that's flowed through me,
it's as if a string quartet is playing—
movements of phrase and variation,
dissonant melodies in search of a theme—
always drawn to the melancholy cello—
miniaturized moments of perfection,
yet when it's over—
nothing but silence hanging in air,
no evidence music was ever there, except,
this sharpened sensibility.
Which must be the way the universe senses,
its agonizing journey toward complexity,
a relentless auguring—particle dust to thought,
from before what's remembered,
to all that's portending.

Peggy F. Brown
Gray, ME

Gift to the Poet's Daughter

I see you sitting there
at the table made of wood
Struggles of life are hard
but you try to find the good

Hardworking man on the farm
and at the mill you slaved
Lived through the Great Depression
showed how honest men behave

Your thoughts were deep
needed to share
important matters of your day
locking time in a moment
before it
...........slipped away

I see you sitting there
at the table made of wood
Struggles of life are hard
but you try to find the good

Your cursive writing flowing free
upon the pristine page
The beauty of your script
Palmer method of your age

Upon the page your thoughts transpired
to a legacy from thee
I hold them now and clutch them tight
thirty years you've been gone from me

Peggy F. Brown
Gray, ME

You captured life I had not lived
as the baby of the fam
Our history's written on the page
just regular, not glam

Now I am sitting here
at the table made of wood
Struggles of life are hard
but I try to find the good

So meaningful to read your words
Riches I did not inherit
but you gave the gift of thoughts to me
Truly glad that you did share it

I now think in rhyme, just like you
Hope to leave words for my kids too
Pen in hand, I write thoughts down
your presence I sense—a hug surrounds

Thank you Dad for filling the page
with the hopes
    and dreams
        and fears of your age

My children hold two books in hand
one from their mom
    and one from her father
        who is their grand

Karen Lewis Foley
Topsham, ME

Autumn Morning, Mouth of the Sheepscot River

How deep the silence; early sun
reaches low light from its rising,
through tall windows on the woods,
through the silence of the house
high above the river, no one else awake,
and warms my face and hands.

How deep the silence beyond; wind
moves through high pines and dry leaves.
Mourning doves lift off on fluting wings.
In the silence a seal croaks
and slaps a rock offshore.
A solitary loon lifts a call across the water.

How deeper the silence in the sounds that rise
beyond the windows—deeper than closed book and
candle flame, cat asleep, heat rising from the stove.
Deeper than sitting very still.

We are borne by the sounds of living things—
water, seal slap on stone, leaves loosing life
into the wind, the speech of loons—into deep silence,
into the heart of the world, borne home.

Sally Woolf-Wade
New Harbor, ME

After the Concert
Monhegan Island

Quarter notes remaining from the Solstice Jamboree
hang suspended from raindrops
as I inch my way down the dark road
from the island church on the hill.

Tunes of fiddle and guitar
circle around my head
repetitively
with the underlying rhythm of the bass.

I remember
the miracle of a French horn
echoing the moan of the island foghorn
transformed into a mournful melody.

I shuffle carefully to avoid
potholes filled with standing water
rippling mirrors of fog
camouflaged pitfalls underfoot.

I regret the absence of flashlight
but no matter, scattered
helpful fireflies dance in the weeds
to light my way.

Patrick T. Randolph
Murphysboro, IL

Spring in Southern Missouri

Plowing the early spring fields,
Sweat from his forehead drips

Down into an open wound on
The back of his swollen left hand.

The solitary breath of the horse,
The sting of the late afternoon sun—

Memories of a spring breeze stroke
The back of his neck—sending

A chill so mysteriously deep into his
Spine that he still feels its nip

Here in this clean, white-walled,
Yellow-curtained nursing home

On this late May day with plump
Mrs. Parker's footsteps coming

Down the almost soundless hall to ask,
"Otis, dear, didja take yur pills yet?"

Emily Ellis
Lewiston, ME

Invincible

From the moment we saw her behind bars, defying someone to reach in and touch her, which of course Robbie did in his 8-year-old glorious ignorance, and thus so aptly named her Nipper, on the spot, we knew she'd be the next member of our family. What we didn't know, and probably would not have believed, not the Ouija board, the Tarot reader, the clairvoyant nor the wisest of the 3 wise men, was that she'd live to be about 17 (that's anywhere from 85 to 119 human years, depending on the breed equivalent). She'd outlive puppies, older and younger "sisters," and human friends, outsmart cruising cars on our busy street by yes!, looking both ways before crossing to chase her fancy, outdo every night sound as she roamed the back woods in pursuit of the live dinner she didn't get at home and out-maneuver whatever obstacle came along her path on the 5-day missing-in-action stint during one frightful balloon festival. That later.

Ours was a family of dog-owners, even prior to our human baby's (Robbie) birth. There was Heidi, the German Shepherd runt of the litter who my father insisted might eat the child if we weren't constantly on guard. Never needed to—she guarded every inch of his space as if he were her own. From the male Siberian who loved the scent of females in heat, or at least warm, almost as much as live chickens, to a succession of black, yellow and chocolate labs, Nipper was our only pound pet as well as the smallest, shortest, sassiest and brassiest. Her papers were never amassed, thus we never knew her lineage, birthdate or first family, just that she was picked up as a stray at a very young age. Could she have gotten away and was following Peter down the hole?

In every way possible, and as those who met her agreed, she looked, sounded, behaved and held her head like a Beagle. Tri-colored, white-tailed, with large, curious, intelli-

Emily Ellis
Lewiston, ME

gent eyes, about 28 pounds in her prime, she would trot as briskly as the bigger girls on the hilly roads we walked and run as spryly in the woods, whatever the season. Unlike the others, she was the one who needed to be leashed before we left the woods on the return home. Otherwise, it was, "Wish me luck guys, I'm going to find that woodchuck if it takes me all night," (sometimes it did) or "...call Connie (our neighbor) in a few hours. I might stop by there—she usually has good eats." On a better day, after a 2 or 3 mile hike, just as we'd be turning the corner of our house, she would scurry across the road, with or without the leash on, and tear for the woods behind those houses. She had no preference for one side of the road or the other or the right bush, the left clump, as long as it held the potential for prey. In fact, it was from one of her forays to the "other" side when she returned home swishing her tail as if she'd won the Miss Lassie contest, with a partial carcass of a deer longer than her entire body hanging from her mouth. Commanded to drop it at the front door she did, but kept on wagging her tail, as if taunting my authority while extending a bouquet.

Naturally she enjoyed sleeping on Robbie's bed with the cozy, blue-print down comforter; loved it so much she ripped it wide open and flooded the room with downy clouds—which I found one day upon returning from work. She was hiding, you think? Rather, sound asleep in the warm white tufts. Another year or 3 later, it was the outrage of Nipper that visited us on November 1st. Matt (our second son) had his candy from the night before tucked neatly under his bed in a sealed plastic bag. We found the bag, holes and all, with scores of wrappers scattered across the rug. In my memory, Nip was stretched out on a doggie pillow in the living room, dreaming of Reese's Pieces and Milky Ways when I rudely interrupted her. Not only did she refuse to look guilty (a sure sign she was), she didn't even get sick!! Maybe we should have investigated her background further.

It was August a few years later. By this time, Robbie had

Emily Ellis
Lewiston, ME

moved onto other activities and didn't have as much interest in his dog. I was in our backyard about to start on a walk down the road with our 2 dogs, when we heard the hssss... hssss getting louder and louder. The sound was followed by the object itself—a huge bright hot air balloon, close enough to the ground for me to see the people inside the basket, giving them the ride of their lives during the Great Balloon Festival of our twin cities. Not wanting my hand to go on its own ride, I dropped the leash as Nipper bolted, through the woods between our house and Connie's. Knowing I'd never catch her on foot, I left the lab at home, zipped into the car and zoomed down the road. No sign of a crazed Beagle or any dog. I turned the car around, pulled over, got out and yelled her name as loudly as I could. More balloons filled the sky with their unmistakable noise. I figured she was gone for good and started mourning. Back home I called neighbors, the vet, animal shelters and the police. We waited.

That night we developed a poster of Nipper's face and upper body with our address and phone printed beneath. A reward for safe return was also included. The next day, after school, Matt and I went to convenience stores, restaurants and animal places within 30 minutes of home and put up signs. Matt helped to keep me focused and motivated. This felt like our mission. Besides the afternoon walk, Frank and I walked the lab at night, Annie perked up her ears whenever she thought she heard a strange sound—she knew her little buddy was missing, could hear the anxiety at least in my voice. Then, on the 5th night, at the corner of our street, Annie started her be-bop dance and began making high-pitched squealing sounds. I called "Nipper" once, twice, and then she answered back in her inimitable raspy bark. As Annie pulled on the leash, we rushed up the opposite street. Frank waded through thick clumps of intertwined brambles and bushes and THERE SHE WAS!! with the leash coiled around some branches and still attached to her collar!! Annie's paws were mid-air, I was ecstatic, Frank felt like a

Emily Ellis
Lewiston, ME

hero and Nipper, uncharacteristically, licked our faces vigorously and seemed relieved. She looked a little leaner, but was uninjured. For days, weeks after, we speculated on where she might have been, how far she traveled, what she ate...She wasn't revealing anything, but every time we stepped outside, she'd tilt her head and eyes upward, ears out at attention, daring those balloons to appear.

Adventures didn't stop there, though there were no more solo flights. One summer the 6 of us hauled off on a transcontinental RV trip to Alaska. From small campgrounds in Ontario and Manitoba to stateside KOAs and friends' driveways before arriving at The Great One, Denali, she found her spot by the couch and sometimes in the passenger seat when we stopped to eat. She easily mastered hopping on and off the steps of the 28' moveable home, eating in a tiny kitchen area or on the ground and adapting her biological needs to human convenience, for the most part. On another trip some years later in the same RV, this time with an additional lab, we were zipping along the Ohio turnpike when I noticed that Nipper kept inching up closer and closer to the front and tried nestling between the two seats. Minutes later, Matt yelled from the back, "Fire! Fire!" As we turned to look, flames were erupting from the side panel. Everyone hurried out while Frank doused the spreading sparks with the small fire extinguisher. Rob called emergency while I moved as far away from the highway as possible and tied the dogs to a tree. Soon came the police, firetrucks, sirens wailing, cars whizzing by and Nipper barking non-stop except when given a treat. The 2 labs watched quietly, letting Alpha dog express their collective indignation. We were supposed to be heading to the Grand Canyon, not Cleveland! But plans had to change radically when we learned the vehicle was totaled because of a mishap with the tailpipe that rendered our traveling woefullies defunct. Camping out at the Red Roof Inn with 2 teenagers and 3 dogs was almost as much fun as me driving back to Maine in a rented Ford Taurus with the Three

Emily Ellis
Lewiston, ME

Stoolies, I mean droolies in the back. Nipper usually convinced me to keep her in the front.

Though some might dispute this, Nipper had her tender moments. When Annie had her litter of 8, it was Nipper who patrolled outside the whelping box. As the pups grew a bit bigger, we allowed Nipper inside the box to lick a pup or 2 while Mama was preoccupied. Are we talking Florence Nippengale? When the pups started vocalizing loudly, she ran downstairs and stayed at their door. When they started standing on their hind legs and peered over the sides, Nip was there to greet them, lick their faces and, when she could, check that they ate all their food (if not, she did). Years later, as Annie aged and her arthritis became more pronounced, she was unable to walk the 2 miles with the others. Did Nipper know she was in pain? Was she able to pick up on those subtle signs that may have escaped human perception and sensibility? When Nipper came back from her walk, she spent hours (it seemed) licking Annie's long yellow ears, inside, outside, top, bottom, left, right, over and over. She also enjoyed mounting Annie's back and doing "the unnatural" as we called it, but it looked a bit like step aerobics and, who knows, it might have helped Annie's stress.

I had not experienced the aging of pets, never having had one as a child. As expected, age slowed Nipper down a little and added some gray to her face. There was nothing much beyond that, except that 2 or 3 years prior to her death, she developed a lump on the top of her front paw. It was small to start with, but grew noticeably every few months or so. Our vet had a biopsy done on one of our visits—it was a tumor—cancerous. We had 2 options: amputate the front paw or wait until the growth bursts on its own, and that would lead to death. Given her age and her relatively healthy life we chose the latter, figuring we might have 6 months at least. While the tumor was unsightly, it didn't seem to alter Nipper's behaviors. She did the stairs fine, still walked almost 2 miles daily (although I found a new trail consisting of some road,

Emily Ellis
Lewiston, ME

some woods and this became our special path), ate the same food in the same quantity, eliminated the same, devoured rawhide treats as usual and in every way acted like the tough queen she'd always been.

In November of her last year, we would awaken early and find an accident in the sunroom—where she usually slept. We attributed this to her advancing age, colder temperatures, the possibility of Cushings disease (though blood work never confirmed that) and just Nipper being Nipper. But soon this behavior led to other disturbing trends. It required more persistent cajoling to get her to take a much shortened walk and when climbing the stairs, her gait was more labored. Sometime in January we noticed her appetite was slacking off. I would put a few kibbles in my palm, call her, and she'd nibble a while and then stop. No matter how or with what I tried enticing her to eat more, she wasn't motivated. Instead, she found a dog bed, lay down and closed her eyes. In addition to a disinterest in food, she wasn't watching the other dogs or us—it appeared that she was disengaged from her surroundings. For the next few days, she was equally disinterested in going outside unless absolutely necessary. Shortly thereafter I called the vet and explained the behaviors. Of all things, the tumor seemed to be bothering her the least. The doctor said it sounded like it could be an intestinal problem and suggested bringing in a "sample." That didn't happen since within a day or two thereafter Nipper stopped eating completely and took only a few sips of water. Her eyes looked glazed and she didn't even seem to notice or care when someone walked right in front of her. This time the vet said she must be seen.

Nipper used to love going for rides, but that day when I tried to persuade her to get in the car, she stood as firmly as she could outside the door. As gently as I knew how, I picked her up. She nipped at my fingers and growled low. She was angry and in pain and nothing seemed to be stopping it. During the 10 minute ride, as she lay on the floor in the

Emily Ellis
Lewiston, ME

back, I told her how sorry I was and that maybe Dr. B. would discover what was wrong. But I knew this was untrue. Nipper was dying and would not be coming back home. That's what they told me at the vet's. She might last a few more days, but her health was only going to get worse. Many systems in the body had already begun to deteriorate—putting her down now might well be the most humane thing to do. Nipper and I were alone together in one of the big visiting rooms where we'd been before for routine check-ups. We sat on the floor, me stroking her head, paws, back, and talking about the many wonderful times we had together. After a while, she got up slowly, moved away and lay down, as if to say enough...enough...this is hard on both of us. Ah Nipper, is that what you were thinking? Ever the pragmatist who knew she lived life fully and solidly and had little time for whimpering.

I'm telling you this now, Nip. When the tech came in, attached the leash to your collar and escorted you out the door, I cried, not only because I was already starting to miss you but also because you walked out as resolutely as you walked into my life. And sometimes I still cry when I look out the window. I see your shadow running in the snow, which turns to green, which gets covered with leaves, which coat this earth in the richest of hues as have you, my dearest, enriched us all throughout the days of your life.

Mary Jo Balistreri
Waukesha, WI

For Sam

(1997-2005)

In Normandy,
among thousands of white crosses,
with the sea's cool sutra
lapping against cliffed rock,
time loses its foothold.
And who is to say
the weighted stillness
is not filled with the voices
of those ever-young men?

In Giverny,
among hundreds of water lilies,
in ponds of mirrored glass,
truth is not fact but reflection.
And who is to say
up isn't down or that the pond doesn't hold
an entire universe?

In big sky country Montana,
millions of white stars
hold up the night sky.
And who is to say
they do not radiate light
into hearts
empty of feeling?

In a small town in Wisconsin,
among two hundred orange balloons
blooming in the blue sky-field
like Monet's Poppies,

(continued)

Mary Jo Balistreri
Waukesha, WI

who is to say
Sam is not present? Or that life
is mortal because the form is final?

Or that the sky, alive with orange,
is not the laughter of a child
clapping his hands
in delight?

***

Winter Over the Pond

Winter's hand cuts into ribbed wood
like a burin, a shivery rattle of good-bye.

Large limbed and nearly naked trees
rattle in the wind against a fire-red horizon

as sun sets and closes the border of day.
Night scratches the trees with frost,

a black and white etching, lines
decisive and stark, everything stripped

to its skeletal essence. Yet in the dead
of winter, resurrection seems possible.

*First published in *Echoes.*

Patricia Goodspeed
Jefferson, ME

Later Chores

a warm November
instead of the usual cold that brings me in
the gray skies hold the empty branches close
the balsam firs the only respite in this stark season
but wait, there on the lawn's slope
the apple has shed most of her fruit
all but the strongest stems still held
to decorate the dark day
and on the ground many yellow globes invite the deer
and leave a kind of mission
in the brown grass

yes, they should be gathered
but I will leave them for the snow to cover
and in this leaving
exercise my power to own
some lingering aspect against the hastening season

for a few months more I'll let them stay
to rake them in the Spring,
and do then what I should do now
remembering this moment
when I take them to the compost pile
gathering my own interior rhyme
scheduled for another day
gifted with these Autumn thoughts
that wish for later chores, arriving,
having tread with hope
the icy path ahead

Genie Dailey
Jefferson, ME

Sunday, Any Day

As if from a steeple,
The buoy bell beckons me nearer the sea—
Salt air for incense; waves murmuring music;
Wild roses adorning the shore.

Congregating gulls and terns, exultant in the sky,
Create a singing, wheeling, sun-blushed choir.
Their soaring robes toss reeling shadows
Over sea and sand and stone
While I drift with their rhythms
And hearken to their hymns.

At the whim of the waves and the wiles of the wind,
The buoy bell's chime comes dancing
Into my reverie.
Adding its harmony to the airs of the choir,
The bell is welcomed, completing the music.

Filled with spirit, the litanies of water, wind, and wings,
The songs of seagulls, terns, and buoys
Lift me above the stones and sand
And sail me into the day.

Carol Willette Bachofner
Rockland, ME

Death, Etc.

Et cetera, and so on—we die
each heading into or toward or under
the wave that surges and then departs.
We cannot hold on longer,
cannot duck out of its way, hide
under the bed. Sooner

or

later, the maestro will tap the baton
raise his arms. The final music will rush
to embrace the whole audience. The orchestra
thrills to each note, braces for the crescendo
that signals the end. As the last notes shake
the place, we rise to our feet and applaud

then

the place empties of all human breath
and the walls go silent, the chairs return full thick,
no imprint of the sitter remaining. The exit
lights glow, red. Et cetera, and so on, we go
where we have been called. A taxi or a bus
waits at the curb. We queue up and wait our turn.

C. Ross Painter
Owls Head, ME

Deep Sea Hand Line Fishing Trip

Every summer from mid 1930 to 1960's our family and friends were treated, by my father Captain Frank Ross Sr., to a deep sea hand line fishing trip. The previous day he would borrow 15 or 20 extra life jackets, rig up hand lines made of a rectangular wooden frame, wound with several fathom of trawl line. He fueled and iced up; laying in a good supply of milk, onions, potato, salt pork and crackers for chowder and cream and strawberries for ice cream, plus plenty of extra snack goodies for munching. Barring a hurricane wind we went, fog, rain or shine, calm or choppy; weather was no problem.

On an August morning at 5 a.m. a group of us stood shivering in a pea soup thick fog on O'Hara's wharf, water droplets clinging like crystal beads to foul weather gear; while waiting to board my father's sixty-five foot fishing dragger *Helen Mae*. Inching along splintery dock planks, we peered cautiously over the edge, at the vessel gently rocking in the low tide water eight feet below.

With pounding heart, one foot was forced over the side onto the ladder, while clammy fingers gripped its algae coated rungs, each foot hesitantly searching for the next ladder rung, then at last an apprehensive leap across deep water gap between dock and boat and finally land on boat deck; vibrating from the heavy engine below.

At sea level dark green water swirled around row upon row of white barnacled-kneed wharf pilings, giving the appearance of soldiers on the march. The damp air smelled of tarred rope, fuel oil, the stench of harbor clam flats and of strong fresh brewed coffee; all combined making one feel a bit squeamish but still comfortably akin with a coastal heritage.

When all were aboard and accounted for, the big diesel

revved up for departure, spewing black plumes of smoke from the stack before blending into the grey mist. Our vessel nudged with a soft thud at cushioned fenders of the outer berthed boats, as we slowly inched backward and forward, then as if on cue, they parted silently to make way for our escape.

After gliding carefully past moored boats in the inner harbor and the fog veiled light of Rockland Breakwater, we slowly picked up speed and passed the shadowy headland of Owls Head Lighthouse, our own squealing fog horn echoing a shrill answer to its distinctive contralto tone two signal.

On a flat ocean swells, bell bouys clanged rhythmically providing a light musical accompaniment to other sea sounds, that of distant multi-pitched fog horns, the muffled drone of several lobster boat engines, our own thundering craft and at our stern the ever present flock of squawking sea gulls searching our churning wake for their morning meal.

Clearing the north east tip of Monroe Island, a narrow rim of red could be seen on the waters eastern horizon, tinting pink an opaque shroud that curtained the offshore islands. Shortly, from the earlier dead calm, a westerly breeze freshened; lifting the low mist from the water's surface; foretelling a perfect day on the ocean waters, as we steamed full speed into Penobscot Bay.

Young children were tethered by rope to the mast to assure no "man overboard" alarm would be sounded. Older folks were seated on blanket-draped hatch covers, and others found their sea legs in short order and were free to roam. Teenagers gathered on the bow, toes inside sneakers gripped the deck while managing to roll with the ship's frantic motion; as she alternately sliced smoothly through deep ocean troths then with momentary halting buck, slam head on into the next six foot swell; sending a geyser of water high into the air. Wind shear and water plastered clothing tight to bodies as stinging eyes were wiped and salty moisture was licked from our lips. Shouting gleefully we braced for the next

C. Ross Painter
Owls Head, ME

drenching.

Later in bright sunshine, with the engine cut our fishing dragger turned into a cruise ship and we drifted leisurely on sparkling blue water. Fish lines were baited and thrown over the side, the first to pull in a ten or fifteen pound bull haddock, would supply the main ingredient for lunch, a huge fish chowder being prepared by my mother and others in the forecastle below.

On deck a flock of eager children stood in line for a turn at hand cranking fresh strawberry ice cream, a party elder supervising the exact portion of salt to ice needed to ensure a perfect icy confection. On the ship's bow teenagers lolled on crew bunk blankets with a battery radio, just passing time until the sun started to dip in the western sky and we began our return trip to home port and the welcoming icy ocean prow-spray that would cool our hot sun burned bodies.

***

Patrick T. Randolph
Murphysboro, IL

Phone Call at 39—Memory at Age Three

Ma's voice on the phone:
Something in its melody,
Its touch in my ear—

My eyes hold vivid pictures,
Ma laughs, sunshine on her nose.

Lauren Meier
Gunnison, CO

Thomas

It happens each time,
He reaches for us,
Embrace him tender,
hugs and kisses passed.

Then Mom and Dad must
leave, happiness drains,
from all of our eyes.
I can't help but cry,
hate leaving my boy.
Need him and he needs me.

Reaching for the door,
he reaches for me,
crying, breaking my,
heart in all pieces.
Hate to leave, Thomas.

Cindy Partington
Dallas Center, IA

After Dark

night falls gently
around us
decreasing our light
by tiny increments
until we notice

our children grow
our faces wrinkle
our muscles weaken
at a snail's pace

a storm builds patiently
lightning cuts through the dark
providing miniscule glimpses
of the reality lingering beyond our senses

we struggle to glean what we can
in those milliseconds of clarity
hoping to get a grasp of
what lies waiting in the dark

Sarah P. Roy
Oakland, ME

Song of Winter

A snowman
with red wool scarf
stands in shadows
moon brought.
Trees give cold witness
to what is coming.

A woman—
still up, did
quietly watch
his cumbersome
movements of dance . . .
become graceful.
Still dressed for day,
she hurriedly put on
a scarf of red plaid.

His rhythm
calls her out.
She accepts with
a curtsy his hand
of branch.
Swirling as leaves
do in fall,
they dance
in silver moonlight
to fantasy's song.

He gently
bends her down
to kiss the snow . . . .

Sarah P. Roy
Oakland, ME

In the frosty indigo
morning, red sun starts
to rise, coldly shines
on two scarves—

one red wool,
the other, plaid.
They hang loosely
around the necks
of two snowmen
in place of one.

Arms of branches
entwine (remaining thus
through spring thaw),
while winter's heartbeat,
as music, sounds a
soprano's highest note—
shatters the silence
of dawn.

Beth Jack
Huntington Beach, CA

Ceremony

We position ourselves
like fragile bookends, so easy to touch
so easy to break.
You turn to light the chandelier
with false brightness, bringing luster
to our formal room,
like a burnished coin under glass.
The upholstery is a rose-bud print,
sofa and chairs all match, an elegant set
as uncomfortable as our last conversation.
We cannot even speak of small duties:
who will retrieve the fruit and cheese
from the kitchen, or wrap the gift
for my father's birthday,
a tasteful watch
with a clever face.

Kathryn Warren
Westfield, NJ

A Cherry Tree Grows in Brooklyn

As the days begin to show signs of spring and I no longer feel captive in the warmth of my home, I have the luxury of these all too few moments of sitting in my backyard. As winter becomes a distant memory, I long for such tranquil days, and my longing for time unencumbered is even greater. So I sit and I stare. And as I do, my thoughts go back to Brooklyn, family, and one enormous cherry tree.

It is a balmy summer day. I am four years old and in my grandparents' Brooklyn backyard, in what was considered to be a very nice section of Brooklyn—East New York. It had to be, for wherever you turned there were families—not just one, but many. I was blessed with a large extended family that included two sets of grandparents, aunts, uncles, and cousins too numerous to count. My most vivid image is that of 34 Georgia Avenue, and the familiar three-story brick apartment house that proudly housed all of us at one time or another. I can still see the dimly lit hallway leading to the back door and to the compact backyard that never seemed as small as it really was.

Grandpa's cherry tree was tucked away in the rear of the yard. Actually, it grew from a neighbor's yard, but since its cherry laden branches drooped into Grandpa's yard, we called it *Grandpa's tree*, and so it was. Only those grandchildren old enough and agile enough were given the chance to climb its shaky boughs and reach for those juicy jewels. Cautiously watching, one of the adults would stand nearby with an empty bowl to be filled with those ruby red cherries. Once the picking began, there seemed to be no end as one, two, and often three bowls would be filled to the brim, soon to be emptied as we'd all pop those luscious cherries into our mouths. Of course, there were pits, but no one seemed to care since they'd be thrown right back into Grandpa's gar-

Kathryn Warren
Westfield, NJ

den. "They're good for the soil," he'd declare.

It's not just the cherry tree I remember. It's everything about those days. It was a yard filled with family, laughter, and plenty of sunshine. It was the steady hum of conversation that resonated through the thick summer air, words mostly spoken in Italian when the adult conversation was not for our impressionable ears. It was cousins playing and cavorting without a care in the world. It was the familiar sight of three tiers of clothes lines (one for each floor) draped above us with freshly washed towels and tablecloths arranged in a well thought-out pattern—but never on a Sunday because no one ever did laundry on a Sunday! It was being outdoors until the mosquitoes were more than we could bear and the skies dimmed to dusk. It was having our day turn into night and continuing the laughter indoors accompanied by coffee, cake, cookies, and more conversation in a kitchen that wasn't much larger than Grandpa's backyard. But that never mattered.

Things matter now and I am no longer that four-year-old girl. There is no tree to climb, cherries come from the store, and cherry pits are carefully thrown away. The children are all adults now with backyards and kitchens that are much more impressive. Family doesn't live around the corner anymore; in fact, some of us live in other states. Days of calling each other and hearing *I'll be right over* are gone and conversations now happen by email.

Some say a child's perspective is quite different from that of an adult. As I write this, I can't help but wonder if Grandpa's cherry tree is still standing or if my family's memories are as vivid as mine. I know these memories that are so much a part of me are mine alone and I cherish them. As thoughts of those glorious times linger in my mind, I will never forget that marvelous cherry tree and those carefree summer days.

Franklin Marshall
Simsbury, CT

Hard Thoughts on an Indian Summer Afternoon

Argument

Certain acts of humankind strain credibility even beyond the play of an unchecked imagination. In Appalachia, especially in West Virginia, coal mining operations lead to mountain top decapitations, where such extreme, consummately destructive landscape remodeling results in an annulment of nature's aesthetic dividend. An orogenic event that evolved over an unguessed measure of geologic time becomes in a matter of months an eyesore vista of rock debris entangled with the residuum of deforestation.

This environmental defilement is not limited to the eastern part of the United States. Gold fever spikes in the western states when mountain dominant tracts, said to harbor deposits of precious metal, are rent asunder by the jaws of strip-mining machinery. Together with the tailings, the chemical solvents used in the treatment of ore, contaminate the circumjacent waterways and spread morbific elements across the water tables, leaving in the wake of profit at any cost, a devastation incapacious of sustaining whatever forms of organic life higher than microorganisms.

When I sort sheaves of language that attest
To ingenuity of proverb craft,
I see birds of a feather at arrest
In foliage finality, A draft

Of weather iron strikes from distances
Far greater than a stone, unmossed, would roll
From buttes, ore sacrificed, to instances
Of rivers, rubble locked, where like a mole,

Franklin Marshall
Simsbury, CT

Squint-eyed and hypogeal, proctors cleave
To silences, ungolden, at the change
To land-loosed, spall-spread legacies. I grieve
What massif murders and repledge to range

Politic forums with a chance to view
An earthwhile justice when the moon is blue.

Blue moon—a fanciful, flowing from
Folklore designation assigned to an actually occurring
lunar event. Blue moon pertains to those rare times
When twice within any given month the moon reaches
a state of fullness, hence the expression: once in a blue
moon.

***

Patrick T. Randolph
Murphysboro, IL

Silhouette

Scarecrow's arms
Hands outstretched—
Holding Full Moon!

Dorothy Weiss
Orlando, FL

Voices

Strolling along the placid shores of the Banana River in Merritt Island, Florida, we were startled by the sudden appearance of two dolphins swimming toward us. We stopped and watched these creatures in amazement. Two pelicans dived from the sky flying over the dolphins' heads matching their movements, circling, flipping, spiraling, disappearing beneath the water's surface and re-appearing soaring up in the air, dripping liquid diamond water droplets sparkling in the sunlight. Two baby manatees joined in this impromptu river dance, floating closer and closer as if they were performing a "water ballet" just for us. We could almost reach out and touch them.

Another onlooker, a man preparing to windsurf was also surprised. He told us that these sea creatures usually stay further out in the water, away from humans.

We had chosen this quiet tranquil inlet because our hearts and minds were heavy. The war in Iraq and the extensive non-stop media coverage had turned our brains to mush. We just felt numb, and wondered, *Is there no hope for the human race and peace?* Depressed, dejected, we had turned our television off, got into our car and driven to this place by the river seeking comfort and quiet.

The playful antics and joyful sounds of these beautiful creatures of nature replaced the heaviness we had felt. They were speaking to us in their own unique way. They seemed to say, "We know how you feel, but look at us; we just keep moving, existing, surviving. Don't give up!"

Observing them, we realized they had given us what we needed most, a change in our outlook on life. They had shared their beauty, their special quality, freely and abundantly, like wild flowers that bloom along a roadside charming weary travelers passing by.

Dorothy Weiss
Orlando, FL

We returned home with our sense of harmony and balance restored. Comforted, uplifted, courage renewed, from having observed sea creatures dancing, singing, frolicking, playing, surviving in the Banana River.

If they can continue to exist, to survive, thrive and dance to the rhythm of life on planet Earth, without fear, so can we.

***

Carol Willette Bachofner
Rockland, ME

Pricked

One drop and her numbers fall
into view. She thinks herself not so fragile
that her islets would malfunction.

Mirror mirror, tell me I am still beautiful.
One drop of blood and my family tree
feels the stir of its sap, generations
feeling the prick, the loss. Who began
the whirl of the spinning wheel,
destiny read a drop at a time? Whose
blood was not strong enough, was too sweet,
not able to withstand ice cream?
One drop of blood from the finger
and Beauty falls asleep.

Deb Brown
Norridgewock, ME

The Call

She calls to hear
that
I'm okay

I am
she's not

News of death
a friend's
youngest daughter

Has her concerned
about her own

She weeps
not for
the one who died

Instead she weeps
for something unknown

"Take care," she says
but really means
stay well, don't leave

"I love you,"
is implied.

Jean Biegun
Two Rivers, WI

Stations of Winter

Here I finish these warmed
leftover beans and feel your
sharp focus on dark County J
where deer always cross.

Here I pause for this robin's egg
soft-blue old bowl and am pleased
we found the whole 30-piece set
under 19 bucks in Grall's antique store.

Here I catch our brave furnace tick
harder than faith itself to coax up
welcomes for you and the kids.

Here I turn on lights while winter's gray
kneels quietly by each window's chill.

Here I wait among photos and shadows
and indoor gleanings and strain
toward the voices I am bound to.

Norma Crosier
New York, NY

Why Can't I Grieve?

I was at my friend Bobbie's funeral in Adams, Massachusetts. It was 2005 and I had driven up from New York City that morning. Bobbie and I had known each other since first grade, and after college, we had both worked in New York at the same time for two or three years, until she married and moved back to our hometown of Adams. We had the kind of friendship that when I visited her two or three times a year, we could pick up right where we had left off as if it were yesterday.

I knew how much I would miss her. *But why didn't I feel the loss more deeply? And why did I not grieve more when others close to me had died in the past few years?*

Sitting there among Bobbie's family and friends, my mind wandered back to the time of my first great loss and I wondered: *Could it be that what I experienced then had been so overpowering that nothing again would ever affect me as much?*

It was Thanksgiving weekend 1950, and I was home from New York for the holiday. My mother was very ill, in the final stages of cancer, and had been bed-ridden at home for the past three months. My dad and sister, Margaret were taking care of her with the help of a nurse who came in for a few hours each day.

We tried to make that Thanksgiving as festive as possible—my dad, Margaret and I, and my mother's sister, Aunt Angie—and it was Mother who insisted that we do everything just right, down to using the best china and linens.

I'd always loved Thanksgiving, absolutely my favorite holiday—the family all together busy with all the preparations for the dinner, breathing in those wonderful aromas, no special obligation except to bring your appetite—but this year was much different. Mother was not with us in the kitchen, guiding us. Every so often, though, one of us would pop upstairs with a crucial question: "Mother, how long do we cook a 14-pound turkey?" and "Do we start basting right away, or wait a while?" She seemed pleased to have some input.

As Margaret and I busied ourselves peeling potatoes and cutting up vegetables, a feeling of guilt crept over me. *Why wasn't I at home helping to take care of our mother, sitting with her, holding her hand? How often had she sat with me when I had the mumps, scarlet fever, one sore throat or earache after another, brought me shredded wheat softened with warm milk, and delicious home-made soup. Now it should be my turn.*

But rationalizing was easy. I had a job in New York and couldn't just take time off, could I? I was secretary to one of the V.P.s at American Airlines and too indispensable, I thought. *I'll get home weekends as often as possible and help out.*

Conversation at dinner was casual. Dad sat at the head of the table and did his usual good job of carving the turkey, and everything tasted delicious. I added some humor with tales of my latest adventures in New York. But our minds were on upstairs, and we took turns checking on Mother and letting her know that the meal was a success. Sadly, she had little appetite for anything other than a clear broth.

The day after Thanksgiving my dad spent the morning at the bank where he worked and returned home at lunchtime. He said he was a little tired and decided to lie down. After a short while he complained of feeling nauseous.

"Dad, can I get you something to settle your stomach?" I offered.

"No, I think I just need to rest a bit," he replied. But very soon he complained of a pain in his chest. I called Margaret from Mother's room.

"Dad's feeling really sick, Marg. I'm not sure what it is but it could be serious. We probably should get him to the hospital. Sit with him while I go downstairs and call an ambulance."

The response was amazingly fast, and I rode in the ambulance with Dad to the local hospital just a short distance away. *Poor Dad*, I thought, as I waited in the emergency room. *What a strain this has been on him seeing his loving wife of 40 years so desperately ill.*

The rest of the weekend was spent comforting Mother, assuring her that Dad was doing okay. I was pleased to report after one of my visits, "Dad looked really good, Mother, had good color and seemed cheerful." Margaret had equally positive news. Getting on my New York bus that Sunday was difficult for me, but we felt good about Dad and I knew I would be back soon for Christmas.

On my trip back to the city, I thought about how kind, gentle and unassuming my dad was. He grew up in Adams, lost his father at an early age, and dropped out of school at 14 to get a job and support his mother. He started in a local bank as a janitor, and would work his way up over the years, step by step until, at his present age of 68, he had reached the equivalent of CFO, second only to the president.

In his early 20's, he met my mother and soon was an active member of her group of friends. He was well-liked and respected by everyone, but even so, he lacked self confidence and felt a little in awe of my mother, whose father was the superintendent of the local woolen mill. But they fell in love and had a long engagement until he had saved enough to buy their first home. There's a wonderful story about the early days of their marriage. According to family lore, my dad was so unsure of his good fortune in having won my mother's hand that, for a brief time after their marriage, he would rush home from work during the day just to make sure she was still there. I always loved that story.

My next few days in New York were pretty routine. The city was decked out in bright lights and a holiday spirit was already in the air. On Saturday, as usual, my two room-

Norma Crosier
New York, NY

mates and I cleaned our apartment, after which I did a little Christmas shopping. I called home one evening and things were pretty much the same with Dad and with Mother.

The following Wednesday morning, my oldest sister, Marjory called me at work from her home in New Jersey.

"Norma, Margaret just phoned me and I'm afraid I have some sad news. Daddy died this morning." I felt a hard knot in my stomach. She continued. "Chuck's mother is going to stay with the kids, and Chuck and I plan to drive home this afternoon. Can you be ready if we pick you up around three?"

Marj had a way of always sounding in full control which she might have felt was part of her job as the oldest child. Six years younger, I was always her "brat" kid sister, while I, in turn, idolized everything about her. After college, she got a job in New York, and six years later, I followed in her footsteps. We became closer when both living in New York, and later, after she moved, with her husband and growing family, to New Jersey.

I managed to say I'd be ready at three, and vaguely remember explaining things to my boss, going back to my apartment to pack a few things, and leaving a note for my roommates.

Much of the four hour drive was spent in quiet thoughts. We were all in shock about Dad. He had seemed to be doing so well the past week. Marj hadn't been home since the summer when she brought her new baby girl to meet her grandparents, and I was able to give her a first-hand report on the Thanksgiving weekend, and a clearer picture of Mother's condition. We found it almost impossible to imagine how Mother would be able to deal with this loss.

Margaret and my Aunt Angie were at the door to greet us. Then Marj and I went upstairs to Mother knowing how much comfort she would need. But she surprised us. She seemed to have mustered up an inner strength from deep within her racked body so that she could comfort all of us. She was sitting up in bed and held out her arms.

Norma Crosier
New York, NY

"Hi, Mother," I said as I hugged her frail body.

"Oh, I'm so glad to see you, dears. You must be tired after your long drive."

"Have you eaten?" were her next words. "Please have something, and then I hope you'll all try to get a good night's sleep. Tomorrow will be a busy day."

Gosh, she sounds almost like her old self, I thought, *with lots of her old energy.* Mother had always been so active, full of life and warmth, with a good sense of humor. Although we were never wealthy, she always wanted the best for her husband and daughters, and felt it important to set the tone socially, making sure we became members of the local country club, and that we three girls had a college education. It broke my heart now to see her so weak and fragile, trying to console us.

The next morning, while Marj, Margaret and I were pondering what to do first, Mother came to our rescue and told us to call Art Simmons, a local funeral director and close friend of the family. She'd been through it all herself when her father died and more recently, her mother. Within a few minutes, Art was at our front door ready to be of help, personally and professionally. Left on our own, we probably would have fumbled our way through, but he took us each step of the way, choosing a coffin, arranging for visiting hours at the funeral home, and the interment. Between us, we decided also to have a church service for Dad since he was so well known in the community, having served as Town Treasurer at one time, and as a member of several local organizations.

All this while, Mother was trying to be her old "take charge" self, giving us her full support and making sure we weren't forgetting anything. "Did you bring a dark colored dress?" she asked me. "I hope your boss understood that you would be away for a few days." We "kids" were all adults, in our late 20's and early 30's, but she still had to be Mother.

Blessedly, once we were caught up in all the details, it

was like just taking one step after another to get through it all, without giving in too much to our feelings. At home, in between more formal responsibilities, we were even light-hearted, telling Chuck stories about growing up in a small town, and always feeling we were rich because our dad worked in a bank!

There is a wonderful custom in small towns at a sad time, where neighbors drop by with casseroles, sliced ham and chicken, cakes and pies—lots of comfort food—and we marveled at how delicious everything tasted. I'm sure if we had had to prepare meals ourselves, we wouldn't have been very hungry. But these dishes, fresh out of the oven, gave us an appetite we didn't think we had.

Only after it was all over did Mother's great strength and spirit start to fade as she gave in to her weak body. We sat with her for a long time Sunday afternoon as she lay there drifting in and out of sleep; then Marj, Chuck and I left, promising to be back soon for Christmas.

At home in New York Sunday evening, my roommates were very comforting, and at the office the next day, everyone treated me extra gently. There was a lot of work waiting for me and I was glad to be busy. Although moments of sadness would come over me suddenly, when least expected, I desperately wanted things to get back to normal. Just nine days later, I had another call from Marj.

"I'm afraid I have more sad news, Norma." She tried to maintain an even tone, but her voice cracked when she added, "Mother died this evening."

"Oh, Marj, no." My eyes filled with tears. After I hung up, I remember thinking: *My gosh, is all this really happening? We just said goodbye to Daddy and now Mother? It's not possible!*

I dreaded telling everyone the latest news. They would be overly kind and I wasn't sure I could handle it. I tried to appear matter-of-fact. I quickly made plans to again meet Marj and Chuck for the drive home, and got away as quickly as I could.

Margaret was at the door and we hugged each other for a long time.

"Oh, Margaret," I said, "what a time you've had here at home." Right now, though, she was calm and just glad to see us. She also had to contend with our Aunt Angie who was never far from tears.

Margaret was the "Rock of Gibraltar" in our family, steady and dependable. We were closer in age and, growing up, had the usual squabbles over whose turn it was to clear the table or wash the dishes, and she often caught me, red-handed, about to go out the front door wearing something from her closet! We even overlapped for two years at Skidmore College. When I was a freshman, and she, a junior, she wisely kept her distance, letting me settle in and make my own friends, but it was comforting during those early insecure days to know she was close by. After college, she chose to remain a small town girl and we saw less of each other, except when I made trips home or when she visited me in New York.

How does one go through a second funeral so soon after the first? Pretty much in a state of numbness, we found. Once more, with Art Simmons' help, we made all the arrangements, and soon found ourselves again receiving visitors at the funeral home. With a double tragedy, everyone felt they must be even more caring, and friends struggled to find the most appropriate words of consolation. Many found it helpful to say, "What a blessing that your mom and dad are together now." And we agreed. It was a lovely thought to hold on to.

As I lay in bed that night, going over the events of the day, and of the last two weeks, I couldn't quite fathom the full impact of what had happened. I must have been in a state of shock because I couldn't even cry.

There were, of course, more home-made dishes from thoughtful neighbors, and we felt the warm comfort of just

Norma Crosier
New York, NY

being together in the home we loved. We made a half-hearted start of going through drawers and closets, but decided this could wait until later, especially since Margaret had decided to give up her apartment in Pittsfield, where she worked, and move back into our family home.

In a few days, we got together for Christmas, this time at Marj's home in New Jersey. We kept busy preparing meals, washing dishes, wrapping presents, not allowing ourselves to think or feel too much. Marj's kids were now age six months, six and nine, so we spent lots of time with them, opening presents and enjoying the excitement of the holiday through their young eyes.

But the next evening, on my bus ride into New York City, as I gazed out the window at the brightly lit houses, I had an overwhelming feeling of loneliness and abandonment. The bottom had fallen out of the warm, secure world that was my family. Here I was, 29 years old, and I felt like a small child, wanting more than anything to have my mother and dad back. When I got to my apartment, both of my roommates were still away. Alone for the first time in many days, I gave in to my feeling of desolation and finally just let the tears flow.

Over the next few days, caught up in the fast pace of the city, I slowly found my life getting back to normal. It helped that my job was challenging and that I had some good friends. I loved sharing an apartment in Greenwich Village.

After a while, I found that stretches of time could go by when I didn't think about my parents. *Perhaps,* I thought, *a time came when grieving ended, when one finally said, "Well now, that's over."* But then suddenly, a chance remark by a friend, "My mother is driving me crazy!" would hit me like a bolt. When my roommate, Joan mentioned one day that her mother and dad were coming to visit over the weekend, I felt a sharp pain of being utterly alone in the world.

I guess there were going to be times like this when I would be overcome with feelings of loneliness; but then, I had wonderful memories to call upon to gently ease the sadness.

My thoughts were drawn back to the present and Bobbie's funeral just as her son, Danny, was telling about the day his mom had won a million dollars in the Massachusetts Meg-a-Bucks.

He added, with a chuckle, "And in spite of this substantial windfall, Mom just quietly made a simple meatloaf for dinner that evening."

Just then, a warm feeling of love for Bobbie's family came over me and, from reliving that brief period in my life many years ago, I discovered how much more fully I was able to share in their loss.

Norma Crosier
New York, NY

John T. Hagan
Kettering, OH

Saddle Pals

In new, soft light of dawning day,
I am often most nostalgic.
Just half awake, I hear you say,
"Now's the time for cowboy magic."
In my mind I load my cap gun,
And I strap on belt and holster.
You'll be there to render child's fun.
My low spirits you will bolster.
You sustained me in my childhood
When my days were long and lonesome.
In backyard West I did what I could
To be daring, brave, and handsome.

Dashing Hoppy, you're so stunning
In regalia all of black.
On grand Topper you'll be running
Toward that fleeing outlaw pack.
With you and Lucky, I'll go too,
And chase those nasty rustlers down.
Their evil deeds they'll surely rue
When they're so slowly marched to town.

On golden mount, good Gene you'll sit.
Champion's fine tack glows and shines.
Faux pistols hang near silver bit.
For such a horse, this young boy pines.
With you and Smiley, I will ride
To catch those crooks who robbed the bank.
From us those culprits cannot hide,
And us a grateful town will thank.

John T. Hagan
Kettering, OH

And you, Roy, are the cowboy king.
You ride; you rope; you shoot the gun.
When time's just right, you'll also sing.
Your daring deeds outshine the Sun.
Together Gabby, you, and Dale
Join the noble strength of Trigger.
With you and them, I'll blithely sail
Through great trials both big and bigger.

Kids now pursue computer games,
And suit the action to their mood.
Their heroes have such hyped-up names.
Imagination gets scant food.
Proud parents kids' lives now refine.
A childhood runs such rapid course.
I wish kids had some friends like mine,
Tough saddle pals who rode a horse.
Old Hoppy, Gene, and Roy and I
Caught all the bad guys of my day.
I wish our kids would now rely
On those who worship more than pay.

Richard Alan Bunch
Davis, CA

Fort Ross in Early Autumn

*[Czarist Russia's trading settlement (1812-1841)
on the northern California coast]*

Cattle in solitude graze in the burnt umbers of autumn
where foam encircles boulders laced with sun-dried moss.

A brisk brine-mingled wind flavors this Mediterranean of
 the sea
cart wheeling over fomented rocks as seals sunbathe.

Fog engulfs the tops of pines in shadowed mists.
Eucalyptus leaves, banana-curved eyes, form beds on the
 forest floor.

A sea otter surfaces a melody's throw away
from a vigilant pelican riding the waves, driven by design.

An erosion-felled tree with its inbred limbs
reaches toward the sea as though vying to find the first
 one.

The horizon blips silver, sun-skipped, gray
on darker gray begins with swells of ropes of kelp.

One gull perched on a rock awash with each sea-splattering
picks apart a glistening fish.

Out at sea, a whitish foam-lane, in plays of a lesser sun,
streaks across that gray mass, brooding with seaweed
 sways.

Richard Alan Bunch
Davis, CA

The cove's sea line laps salt over lusts of sand
where half-life shells beckon, sirens of an unfeigned
fortissimo.

With force and voice these touching membranes
play to shifting lights, murmur textures that color.

***

Patrick T. Randolph
Murphysboro, IL

Aunt Meg's Song

Dad always tells the story of Aunt Meg,
How she'd kick her short leg up in the air
And let a genuine rich old fart smack
The ears and noses of everyone on
That hot summer Iowa farm—even cows
Would teeter and totter after the blow.
Old Aunt Meg would smoke her pipe, laugh a bit,
And when the moment was right, well, she'd lift
That left leg of hers and hurl a wind storm
So powerful the green corn leaves would cringe
And prepare for a Midwest tornado.
Dad says that Aunt Meg's farm is no longer,
But if you stand where the house used to be,
Her mighty song roars as loud as the sea!

Judian James
Camden, ME

The Low-Tide People

The low-tide people
walked the beach,
mingling, lingering

some lagging in
small groups

others,
trooping along at
a faster pace,
as if to race the
tide coming in,

yet, all begin
to search:

for a shell that will
tell the story
of this day
on a windowsill
tucked away,
back at the house
until,
a visiting grandchild
will ask to take
it away to the city

Judian James
Camden, ME

or, a pretty beach stone
uniquely worn, in
shape and tone,
plucked to be saved
as everyone raves
about it when found.

Perhaps, a garnet colored
piece of glass from the sea,
washed smoothly
over time,
as it eventually
made its way to shore.

Treasures all,
as testimony once more
that the low-tide people
do not just roam

the proof's in their pockets
when they return home.

Anne Johnson Mullin
New Harbor, ME

Unsuspected

Water escapes through cracks
in rock faces blasted out
when the highway was
routed through.

Warm weather seepage
barely shows a glint
on fractured surfaces unless
the sun is just right.

But, oh, when days run dark
and cold, how the volume
of bright ice amazes, caught
mid-cascade, hanging mass

of frozen swords color-shot
with secret minerals. Shocking
how beautiful, dangerous rage
bursts from impassive stone.

Rosemarie Nervelle
Camden, ME

On the Inside

The dark side of my eyelids, my side, comforts me. The images appearing there are memories, familiar and dear to me. I know them by heart and they make me happy. I feel myself smiling, sometimes laughing aloud although my face remains rigid. Tears, too, go unnoticed by others. When my eyes are closed, I recall my family photographs, and the images of my beautiful wife whenever I wish; and so, my eyes are closed most days. Periodically forced open against their will, each eye is searched with a bright light, then mercifully allowed to close once again. During these brief invasions, a frighteningly intense face, close, ridged and porous, insinuates itself on my pupils, leaving a negative after-image on the inside of my lids. It quickly fades. I grimace again and turn away. At last, I am left alone to choose whatever memory photos I care to see.

On the outside, there are noises all around, the bustle of people coming and going, clatterings, yelling and talking in languages I don't understand. It is a foreign place of people I don't recognize when my eyes are temporarily open. The scene is morbidly depressing, frightening and hopelessly unchanging. Each time I observe the same activity around me, I squeeze my eyes tight and escape. An intense, worried face appears from time to time. I open my eyes because he's saying something to me in a language I don't understand. He gives me a piece of paper; it's green, there is a man's picture on it and the number one. He points to it and says "dollar bill." I have no idea why he's giving it to me. I don't need it. There is no place to write on it. I tear it in little pieces and hand it back to him. He shakes his shaggy head and goes away accompanied by others dressed the same way. I close my eyes and all is lovely again.

Inside, my eyes watch the sparkling, blue lake just out-

Rosemarie Nervelle
Camden, ME

side our cabin door. My mother is preparing lunch, or is it my wife? No, it's before I married. I'm a child. My two older brothers are swinging on the tree rope and yelling before they drop into the lake. They beckon me, but I'm afraid. Mother comes to the door and sees that my brothers are calling me to join them. She gathers me in one arm and latches on to the rope with the other. We swing clear of the bank and plunge into the lake. It's exhilarating. Mother holds me tight. We surface, laughing. Afterwards, I plunge in like my brothers.

A dark, transparent curtain descends over my eyes during one of those summers. We are at the lake again and my Dad is with us for one whole, glorious week. He bought us a sailboat and is teaching us to sail. We've had a beautiful day, and we're bringing the boat in to shore. I don't see the rusty tin can with its raw lid in the shallows. I scream when I see the blood billow out from my foot. Miles away from the nearest hospital, Dad puts my foot to his mouth and draws out the poison as if I had been bitten by a snake. He spits it out in bloody threads into the water, and I'm awe stricken that he knows exactly what to do.

I'm being moved to another place. I can feel my body lifted and I open my eyes for an instant. It is a room like no other I've ever seen. The walls are draped. A light is over my head. I close my eyes again . . . And there you are! We're walking through a wood, picking blueberries. The sun's warmth is all around us and mingles with our own body heat. Within sight, a pine grove beckons in whispers on the breeze. It's lovely, fragrant and cushioned with years of soft, fallen pine needles. We make love there. Our son Jason is conceived and we know it immediately. Our happiness is unrestrained and we carve our initials, and Jason's name in the bark of a big pine tree we'll always remember.

Our lives with Jason are precious, happily fulfilled and over so soon. He places a child in my arms whose name is the same as mine. I think it's Jason, and you tell me, no, the

Rosemarie Nervelle
Camden, ME

child is Jason's own son. We are his grandparents!

I open my eyes to the face of the worried man. He holds my hand awhile and murmurs something to a woman dressed in white. There are strange gurgling sounds coming from somewhere inside my chest. I am very tired and wish to close my eyes again. The man speaks to me once more. I can tell by his eyes that his words are kindly. My own eyes watch the door to the room. I suddenly smell the familiar perfume you always wore. You speak my name, stroke my hair and kiss my cheek. I know that voice, that face, those lips. I know that you are someone I love, but I don't know your name. I tell you silently that I love you. You whisper something that makes me smile. My eyes dim, and your sweet face slowly fades. Then, reaching down with warm, gentle fingers, you close my heavy lids . . . forever.

***

Liz Moser
Baltimore, MD & Phippsburg, ME

The Burning Bush

Why me,
why now,
what good would it do,
why do I have to?
I'm no Moses.

Marc Seifer
Kingston, RI

The Junkyard Man

He had the belly the shape of a tow truck tire.

Sloshing through seventeen inches of muck
to get me a rear view mirror,
the Santa Claus-sized junk man meandered
overaroundand inbetween
the rusted crashcan cars
and parts.

Kerosene-heated by pungent forced air
his unmoved non-mobile trailer closed
off the cold and served
as a meeting ground
for his mud-adorned troupes
and those like me who came to buy.

I remember the wall calender.
A large round bare-breasted
blonde gal with boobs
that dr$_{oo}$ped below the gritty page.

NOVEMBER 1943 - AUGUST 1981

Twas yesterday I returned
to chew the fat
with the friendly junk man
to beat the game and
save a $buck.

The place was spiffed.
The mud erased.

Marc Seifer
Kingston, RI

A Brand New Trailer
& wire fence.

NO TRESPASSING beyond
this point.

No meandering overandaround and inbetween
the rusted
crashcan cars.

The pretty nice girl
sat
in front of a phony
brick façade.

$2.12 for a Datsun radiator cap,
wrote the neat junk sec'ty.

"Here, forget it," the fat man
used to say.

"Hey, where's the big guy?"
"Died."
"Old?..." I stumbled.

"38 with 5 kids. The two brothers
and four sisters
have it now. But we're closing.
Tomorrow's the last day."

"What happened?" I asked sadly.

"Niel choked to death
on a piece of meat."

Suzanne Collins
Sedona, AZ

To My Hand

You are shaped like my father's
achieving square hand
not my mother's tapered fingers and nails;
with you I raised four children,
a household of six, for thirty years,
pulled a tick from a daughter's head,
pressed a thorn from a tiny foot,
felt the silky softness while brushing hair.

You caressed newborn kittens, then cats,
dogs, lovers and husband,
sculpted clay into images,
scattered seed into vegetable beds,
pulled a thousand weeds,
met a thousand strangers and shook all their hands.

Now, I see you wrinkling with age;
veins protrude, brown spots emerge,
but you carry the glowing rings of appreciation
from one who long ago asked simply,
"May I hold your hand?"

Anne L. Hess
Stillwater, ME

The Coonish Cat

She walks regally with her ostrich-feather of a tail held high, proud and straight except for the question mark curl at the tip, striding as if she were the queen carrying her royal scepter. The only sound she makes is the soft pad-pad-pad of her feet against the hardwood floor as she walks towards the sunlit window where she perches watchfully within sight of her unknowing royal subjects. The cat is disdainful of the birds' cries for more seed, and they give no import to her visage behind the glass, but she attends to them as if their lives depend on it—as any queen should do for her minions.

We've never told her she isn't a pure-bred, blue-blood Maine Coon cat—a breed descended from those feral creatures of the woods and meadows of our once-wild state, and allegedly of Viking origin. We didn't want to hurt her feelings, so proud is she of her long, silky thick black fur that wafts joyfully when she runs. It crowds itself wildly between her toes, and the spritely tufts of fur spray off the ends of her ears like little rockets. In bright sunlight, you can just barely detect the faint gradations of color from mink brown to midnight black. The full-blooded Coon cat would have similar mottling, but there might be white, tawny buff or gray in the mix.

She is only part Coon cat by inheritance, but totally Coonish in her behavior. She, like a raccoon, may wash herself with water before eating. This she does by splashing her paw—usually her left—in her water dish until the table top is quite soggy. Perhaps she is just sloppy as she drinks from her sodden paw, not at all dainty as a proper queen should be. But then, she hasn't had a proper upbringing since I'm not an authentic queen's lady-in-waiting.

Of the four cats I've served, she's the only one I know who seeks out a bath. She will follow close behind me in the

Anne L. Hess
Stillwater, ME

morning as I go upstairs after breakfast, then sit just outside the bathroom door while I take my shower. She taught herself to push open the unlatched door as soon as I step out of the tub. While I stand there shivering before I can dry myself off, she walks up to me and meows expectantly, in that sweet, soft, kitten-like tone that she never grew out of. If I don't respond immediately, which I may do with malice aforethought so I can bear perverse witness to her crafty moves, she will reach up from her hind legs and touch me on my leg with her paws, the goose-bumped leg which is still covered with drips of rapidly-cooling water. She will remain there until I wrap the towel precariously around my nearly-freezing body and gingerly reach down and pick her up.

She doesn't want to be held too long. She leans out of my arms onto the sink shelf, where she will contort and pace until I take my washcloth, still warm and damp from my bath and filled with the smell of my newly-cleaned self, and wipe her gently but thoroughly from head to tail. She may lie down in the sink's bowl and lean her head back to catch the drips from the incontinent faucet; it doesn't even matter if there is a little water in the bottom of the basin. Her daily ablutions are not complete until I have diligently brushed her fur—head and chin, back and sides, belly and tail—with what used to be my own hair brush. Once suitably coiffed, she will jump down to the tile floor with the grace of Baryshnikov, content to seek her bed of the day.

She is smarter than she should be for a creature with such a little brain. At an early age she acquired the ability to open cabinet doors by pulling them with a paw. She thinks the dog brings the meals by her ostentatious snorting, sneezing, and pacing. She knows how to con me out of a sip of cream. She knows how to torment the dog by rushing ferociously at her head, then veering off at the last instant to miss her by an inch; or hurl herself with a billiard-ball bounce off a stuffed chair right in front of the old dog's grizzled snout. Ms. Coonish has taught us to let her upstairs, to clean her litter box or any other task, by leading us where she needs us; there she stands and looks up expectantly. If I try to avoid her request, she will walk in front of me and block my way. She must think, *My servant is lazy today,* or some such thing.

She is no appreciator of music, however. The sound of the tenor recorder in the hands of this semi-novice is tolerable; she ignores it and I practice undisturbed. The high wail of the soprano recorder is too much; I suspect that she thinks I am torturing one of her relatives to death whenever I play it. At those times, within seconds she comes into my practice room, reaches her paw up to my lap and gives one of those haunting, plaintive meows. I stop, pick her up and reassure her for a moment then sit her down. She leaves the room. I resume my playing, only to have to repeat the comforting routine every minute or less. When I despair, I carry her halfway upstairs, where she insists on leaping down to climb the rest of the way herself. I let her through the folding doors, close them and go back to my practice. Usually, that assuages her angst, and I am left to warble in peace.

This Coonish cat clearly was genetically programmed for the outdoor life, but seems not to mind too much that she has to appreciate it from behind the mysterious, invisible barrier that keeps out the wind and the rain. Maybe she doesn't really know that outdoors is different, a separate universe to which she could have escaped if she'd tried. She knows that the dog gets to be out there with us, but she proudly knows she isn't a dog. The huntress in her remembers that, when she was just a kitten, she cornered a wayward mouse between the maple floor and the heat register. She has forever since been a devoted fan of the clicking of the registers, and sits for hours in unwavering vigilance. These days, her largest prey is a trapped-inside housefly or moth. If it hovers too high, and won't come close enough for her to snag, she cries out for me to come and knock it down within her reach. We're quite the deadly team, a sure hazard for the

Anne L. Hess
Stillwater, ME

uninvited small visitor.

Otherwise, she's an angel, a role that came easily for her as the follow-up to the Cat-From-Hell that lived with us previously. She'd rather snuggle than struggle, rather talk than attack, rather follow than ambush, and be loved rather than victorious. I think she's a Democrat.

Little Miss Coonish, aka Her Royal Fluffiness, enjoys a good conversation with the best of us. Just like the talking gorilla or African parrot, she has an extensive cat-abulary that consists of a medley of meows, mews, mehs, mees, hums, burrs, cheeps and chirrs. She growls at the neighbor's car or the UPS man. Then there's the tilt of her head, the half-open eyes, the unwavering stare, the swish of the tail or the waving of a paw; American Sign Language it's not, but her signs are exquisitely expressive. She doesn't bark, yet, but there's still time.

Cats scorn dogs, we suppose, because the creatures are so indiscriminate in their food habits. Those ignorant canines will eat anything: fresh or rotten, animal or vegetable, wet or dry. Not for HRF, however. Fresh, rare meat is preferred; freshly-cooked wild Pacific salmon is a fine delicacy appropriate for Her Fluffiness' epicurean palate. Canned things are, well, better than nothing when you're hungry enough; but no self-respecting carnivore of Viking descent would ever deign to allow a vegetable to touch her tongue.

Which convinces us that our cat can't be pure Maine Coon cat: She loves her leafy green vegetables. She will hungrily sniff, paw, chew and even sinuously roll in freshly-grown grass of any and all varieties. When her indoor miniature lawn of rye, wheat and catnip died off in the heat last summer, she discovered lettuce. Dark green, crisp lettuce done in a chiffonade and sprinkled on top of her meat entreé. Romaine tips are preferred, but iceberg or Boston Bibb will do. Green and crunchy is required.

Who knew? Only the royal cats, I suppose, those with pure Coon blood and undisputed coonly habits.

F. Anthony D'Alessandro
Celebration, FL

What's Wrong With America?

What's wrong with America? George (the First) Bush rallied around his thousand points of light speech, Obama's rhetoric dealt with some sort of audacity of hope. Obviously, these are lifelong politicians and any thoughts of sincerity should not be ascribed to them. Even if we lived in a perfect world, and silver tongued statements made during their presidential campaigns rang true, this nation would be just as troubled.

The fact is, America's problems are not about the Bush Presidencies, nor are they about Obama. Our difficulties are as simple as poolside chairs. That's right. The problem centers around commandeering chairs and allegiance to a me first mentality. America's front row seating obsession has nothing to do with political theory. It's not about Republicans, Democrats, nor is it about Conservatives and Liberals. This epiphany first smacked me directly between the eyes while relaxing on a cruise ship somewhere on the restless Atlantic Ocean.

Since I'm an early riser, I strolled to the ocean liner's pool deck before sunrise, choked my cup of coffee as tightly as a newly discovered sunken treasure and plopped. I read for nearly an hour, barely an arm's length from the ship's pool. Soon after sunrise shyly peeked from behind a clutter of clouds, the stealthy march of vacationers paraded past me. They whispered past me in silence and they worked independently and efficiently. This quiet band of carriers, arms brimming with towels and artifacts, tiptoed around me and placed their embraced items on lounge chairs near the pool. One cruiser had the audacity to inform me of his proprietary claim to my chair since he'd occupied that same lounge the previous day. I suggested he take his gripe to the captain's court.

F. Anthony D'Alessandro
Celebration, FL

Despite this aggressive crowd that would make professional wrestlers look like choir boys, the chauvinist in me dismissed this selfish behavior as an international problem. I rationalized that many of the cruisers were not citizens of the USA.

Recently, I booked a timeshare hotel in the south of Florida. Again, I rose early to sip my eye opening coffee. Since my room perched directly above the pool, I had a clear view of both pool and ocean. I chose to start my day on my room side balcony. Before I finished my first cup of java, a familiar phenomenon unfolded. An army of tight lipped towel carriers invaded the resort's pool deck below. These towel brandishing troops buried pool chairs under an avalanche of towels.

One woman brazenly covered four poolside chairs. That small claim, however, proved short lived, since her companion came out a few minutes later. He blanketed another five prime pool view lounges with the flair of a chef placing finishing touches onto his culinary masterpiece. The man placed a dollop of beach shells and a flowery toy pail on a corner chair, a ragged, coverless book on another, separated a pair of sandals and gently tucked them on nearby chairs, and put a bright yellow shovel that looked like a toy on steroids onto another poolside lounge.

Directly below my patio, a spindly legged preteen hustled over and covered another six lounge chairs. As he started to scramble away, I heard a screech as loud as any mountain yodel. It came from the verandah next to mine. The sunrise hour didn't matter to these vacationing vocalists. With twin foghorn shouts, the boy's mom and dad reprimanded their cover up boy and ordered him to redo his chairs with a more secure coat. He tied those white towels to his claimed chairs like a tourniquet. His territorial claim secured, those covers sat ready to take on any hurricane. It seemed obvious that signs about not saving chairs proved ineffective deterrents to this cavalcade of chair conquistadors. To my surprise, hotel

F. Anthony D'Alessandro
Celebration, FL

employees too remained mysteriously mute throughout invasion of the towel troops.

Even if the political platitudes about hope and points of light miraculously evolved into sincere ideals, we will only dream about those ethical principles. Until we control greed and selfishness, not by edict or federal laws, but by our selfless internal values, we'll remain a selfish society. Sorry, but there won't be hope of uplifting this, or any society, until citizens stop thinking about the "me" above all else, and consider the "us."

***

Hugh Fox
East Lansing, MI

A Little Hole

A little hole in the ice next
to my shanty, loving just
walking across the ice, out
walking my (dead cattail
shoreline) dog, no bombing
any marketplaces, mosques,
cathedrals, anyone, of course
thawtime equals boattime,
immersion in another kind
of existentialist combativeness.

Earl Weigelt
Winslow, ME

Umquenawis

What bulk and brawn and hide and bone
and hump and bell and muzzle!
Now crashing and snapping, an ominous brute;
now silent and soft as a mouse.

Come Spring a forlorn—even comical fellow
dehorned and in shed most ragged
with patches of hair in places all missing,
sheepish he seems in his scratching.

But in Autumn, take care! Pay heed and look sharply,
for then in his shine and his prime,
his strength is unmatched and his temper unruly
and he'll charge and he'll stomp on a dime!

Wading or swimming, feeding or stalking,
brooding or dredging or browsing,
it's *his* time he keeps, make no mistake;
It's *his* ground he walks in the gloaming.

Perhaps you've seen in some dark alder brake
where he's tantrum'd and fussed and he's fumed,
with hoof prints sunk full twelve inches deep
and green trunks all battered and blasted!
Well, some errant twig insulted his eye,
or he caught foreign scent in his snoot,
with sheer tensile force he hooked on those trees
and clear lifted the things from their roots!

Earl Weigelt
Winslow, ME

You might think that he's daft, even numb as a post
but hunt him, you'll soon figure better.
Or startle him, challenge him, trespass his court
and old Monarch will teach you a lesson!

Yes, here in the North, the Great Moose is king,
majestic and massive and free.
God's great woodland beast, the greatest of all—
Umquenawis, the Bull of the Woods!

***

Lorraine Jackson
Detroit, MI

Thankful

I appreciate life in the blink
Of an eye could have been gone.
Having been near death and allowed
To return, My understanding things would
Be different if I wasn't blessed with a second chance
Of life's lessons to learn

No one's life is perfect yet in daily living
Be thankful for the life you have been given.

Steve Troyanovich
Florence, NJ

the stars awake alone

for Elizabeth

each star
roamed eternity
seeking your warmth...
cover me now
with the springtime
in your lips
time loses its winter
on the blossoms of your smile

***

somewhere still yesterday

for Linda

somewhere the sea ends
time ends
love ends...
faded memories
cascade through
lamenting moonlight
our dreams remain
lovers' ghosts
from that other shore...
so lovely in the moonlight
so lonely in the moonlight

Charles O. Boldreghini
Collierville, TN

Fishing With Old Rosella

I remember many things about the summers I spent with my widowed grandmother at her country store and home in the southwestern corner of Shelby County in West Tennessee. But the day I spent on the banks of the Mississippi River with Old Rosella stands out above the rest. The year was 1929. I was seven.

Old Rosella was a small, spry Negro woman who lived alone in a two room shack on Isaac's Knoll which was one of two Negro hilltop communities just to the north of Grandmother's property. The men in these communities made up most of the labor force at nearby sawmills and lumber yards along with a hardwood factory. They and their families provided the bulk of the trade at Grandmother's store. Old Rosella was a part of that trade too. And that's how I came to know her.

I met her one hot afternoon in June of that summer of 1929 when she stopped by Grandmother's store on her way home from a day of fishing at the river. Aunt Louise was minding the store that day and I happened to be in the store enjoying the cooling effects of an ice cold grape soda.

I'd seen Old Rosella many times at a distance, but this was my first close up look at her. Her small, dark eyes quickly moved over me as she told Aunt Louise what she wanted.

I didn't hear what was said. My eyes and mind had quickly shifted from her to the fishing gear and string of fish she'd left on the porch. Quietly, I slipped out the front door and sat down on the porch beside the fish.

A few moments later when Old Rosella came out she said, "Didn't have much luck today. Just them two little four pounders."

"They look plenty big to me," I said, still eyeing the fish.

"I caught a two footer last summer. Almost more than I

Charles O. Boldreghini
Collierville, TN

could do to haul him in."

I stared wide-eyed. "Two foot long! I sure wouldn't want to hook one that big."

Old Rosella smiled as she stepped off the porch. Then, after she shouldered the cane fishing poles and the fish string and took a couple steps toward the road, she half-turned toward me and said, "If it's alright with Miz Maria, you can come fishing with me sometime if you want to."

I sat looking after her as she ambled along the street toward the dirt road that ran up to the Isaac's Knoll community. I was thinking of Grandmother and how she wouldn't let me go anywhere alone off her property. "You're too young," she always said. "The lumber yards and Nonconnah Creek'll still be there when you're ten." I figured there wasn't much of a chance she'd let me go fishing at the river with Old Rosella. But back in the store, as I finished off the rest of the grape soda, the little voice in the back of my mind, egged on by the thought of hauling in a catfish the size of those she had today, kept whispering, *Maybe*. Finally I timidly put the matter before Aunt Louise.

Aunt Louise eyed me for a moment before she said, "Old Rosella's a good woman. And Mama likes her." She smiled, and rubbed my head. "Yeah, I think Mama'll let you go fishing with her."

It took me several days to work up enough courage to ask Grandmother. Finally I found the nerve to do it late one afternoon while she was in the middle of making supper. I was hoping she'd be so busy she'd say yes just to get rid of me. But instead she paused in putting batter on cuts of round steak and looked at me.

"Did she ask you?" she said eyeing me.

"Yes'm" I said, my heart in my throat.

"When?"

"Last week one day," I said, the words tumbling over one another in my eagerness to get them out, "when she came in the store."

"Well," Grandmother said as she continued the breading, "if Old Rosella don't mind having to bother with you, there's nobody I'd sooner trust you with than her."

I stood for a moment with my mouth agape. I couldn't believe it had been that easy. Then I put my arms around her waist from behind and hugged her tightly.

After a moment, she shooed me out, saying, "Get on now, and let me finish gettin' supper."

Old Rosella's fishing spot was at the upper end of a deep backwater pocket that washed up against the concrete foundation of an abandoned gravel plant's dredging tower. The pocket had once served as a loading bay for the huge barges that haul freight up and down the river. In the years since the gravel plant was abandoned, the rapid flowing river swirling in and out of the pocket as it passed, had gradually filled the upper end of the bay with driftwood. And it was there in the deep, still water beneath the driftwood that Old Rosella fished.

Immediately after we arrived on the bank of the bay, and before she laid down her fishing gear, Old Rosella took hold of my shoulders and made me look at her. "I want you to stay aside of me unless I tell you you can go somewhere," she said.

I nodded. She spun me around facing the river. It glistened in the sunlight less than a hundred feet away, and was flowing so smoothly and swiftly its surface appeared solid. I could see an island in the hazy distance.

"You can't play around and swim in that water like you do Nonconnah Creek. If you was to get to playing on that bank yonder and fall in, the river'd suck you down, and you'd be gone. So mind what I say."

She let me think on that while she laid out the fishing gear. Then she handed me the bait can. When the baited hooks had settled into the deep recesses of the water beneath the driftwood, and the cane fishing poles were each secured to a small log on the bank, Old Rosella guided me to an elevated spot of land that was shaded by the gravel plant tower. It was reasonably cool there next to the damp concrete wall, and it afforded a clear view of the area where the bright red corks were moving slowly back and forth in the undulating waters of the pocket.

After several minutes of silence Old Rosella asked how old I was.

"Seven," I said, my eyes were on the corks. I expected one of them to be yanked under any minute.

"I weren't much older than you when I used to go fishing on the old River back when I was a slave living on a big plantation out east of Memphis," she said. Then sensing that she didn't have my full attention she paused before saying, "There was wolves in the river bottoms then."

"Wolves," I said, jerking my eyes from the corks.

Old Rosella smiled and leaned back against the concrete wall while she told me of her life on the plantation, and about the Civil War and on after the war when she married and tenant farmed with her husband while they raised a family of eleven children.

I had forgotten all about the corks until she suddenly stopped talking and said, "Keep a watch on those corks while I go to the other side of the gravel plant and take care of business."

When she got back, taking my cue from her, I asked if I could go take care of business beside the huge sand pile about a hundred feet inland. After I finished my business, I stood eyeing the top of the sand pile. I was torn between the desire to climb to the top of the sand pile and see how far I could see and the urge to go back to watching corks. I quickly came to the conclusion that more than half the morning was gone without one cork disappearing from view. There seemed to be no need of me spending the rest of the morning watching floating corks. Anyway, Old Rosella was watching them.

Charles O. Boldreghini
Collierville, TN

"Can I stay here and climb the sand pile?" I hollered at Old Rosella.

She nodded and hollered back, "Don't you get outta my sight."

The next half hour passed quietly while I sat atop the sand pile pretending to be an Indian lookout. Then suddenly, I heard Old Rosella yelling, "Little Charlie! Little Charlie!"

I looked toward the spot where I'd left her. She wasn't there. I scrambled down from the sand pile and ran toward the sound of her voice as she called, "Hurry, Little Charlie, hurry!"

When she came into sight she was down on her knees at the edge of the bay hanging onto one of the fishing poles with both hands. The top half of the pole was stretched out flat atop the driftwood. All of the fishing line was under water. The small log the pole was tied to had been moved down the back toward the water.

"He's a big'un," Old Rosella panted, when I reached her side. "If I hadn't got here and stopped him he'd a pulled that log on into the water." She paused to catch her breath. "I got him now though, but I can't haul him in. Run get the spare coil of fish line and tie one end to the log."

With the line secured around the log and me and Old Rosella tugging away together, we soon had all of the fishing pole and part of the line on the bank.

"Now, you go and take hold of that pole," Old Rosella said.

I obeyed, but as soon as the line grew taut the fish began to tussle and pull. He jerked the pole out of my hands. When I moved to pick it up Old Rosella said, "Leave it for awhile. Let him wear himself down."

As soon as the line grew slack, Old Rosella said, "Come take hold of this line now while I go get hold of the pole."

When Old Rosella tugged on the fishing pole line, the fish began to tussle again, but she held him easily. "He's tired a fighting," she said. "Come on over here and we'll haul him in

Charles O. Boldreghini
Collierville, TN

together."

The line stayed taut as we moved steadily further and further up the bank. I watched breathlessly as first the red cork appeared and then the large nut Old Rosella used for weight. When the huge head broke the water's surface my eyes popped.

A few moments later the fish lay outstretched on the bank with its whiskers and tail still moving. Old Rosella plopped down beside it and marveled, "That there's the biggest fish I ever caught." Then she looked at me. "I could'-na caught him without your help, Little Charlie. He's our fish. Yours and mine."

Later as Old Rosella labored homeward with the big fish slung over her shoulder, I walked behind her, studying his big mouth and long, thick nose whiskers, thinking, "Wait'll I tell the boys at school about this."

Byron Hoot
Wexford, PA

The Essence of Presence

There's nothing like the way
A deer gives order by its
Presence silhouetted on a hillside
Or stepping between two trees
On an edge line:
          The deer
          Makes pristine
          How well everything
Suddenly fits.
There's nothing like the way
A deer gives order by its
Presence silhouetted on a hillside
Or stepping between two trees
On an edge line:
          The deer
          Makes pristine
          How well everything
Suddenly fits.

***

Giving Up Divinely

Do you think
A tree wants
To keep its leaves
Forever?

Maureen Anaya
Berwick, ME

Start of Another Day

Hark! Hark!
The dogs bark.

Early in the morning

They run about,
Till I let them out.

Early in the morning

The cat meows on and on
I wonder if it's really dawn.

Early in the morning

Awake now, I sip coffee from my cup,
Pets are asleep and I'm up

Early in the morning

Nancy Hungerford
Riverton, CT

The Gray

I once owned a horse farm in Connecticut where we taught dressage in the indoor riding ring and boarded horses. The trails through the Connecticut hills were available for those who simply wanted leisurely, mind clearing rides.

Our horses were thoroughbreds, each with individual traits we learned to appreciate. Feinson, a rust colored horse would nuzzle Blitz, our red Irish Setter who loved to run alongside with him while he carried riders on the trails.

Two others bonded with Petunia, our Nubian goat who would frolic with them in the pastures. She was an offspring of Robert Frost's goats and had the physical attributes of a young fawn, except for her long cocker spaniel-type ears. She'd display her goat moments when she would manage to jump on the roof of our house and imagined she had climbed a mountain.

A pair of Lipazzans, direct off-springs from the horses General Patton saved during WWll, tended to keep to themselves. Perhaps they felt they were more elite than the thoroughbreds. Even though they were still gray and not old enough to attain their white coat, their attitude indicated they believed they'd make their debut at the ritual riding event in Vienna.

The array of barn cats attended to mouse patrol, each finding a cozy, warm straw nook among the horses.

Hubert, our dressage instructor was a talented German-trained equestrian. In addition to his formal riding and teaching skills, he had the ability to run his hands over the body of a horse and recognize all the animal's perfections or flaws.

As the riding business grew, we needed additional horses.

We read in an equestrian publication that horses were for

Nancy Hungerford
Riverton, CT

sale at a reputable upstate New York farm, so Hubert and I drove there to look at them.

We arrived early in the morning just when the horses were turned out to pasture.

That was when I saw The Gray. A frisky young stallion who had been confined to the barn due to a severe snow storm.

When he was released from his lead line, he pranced, ran, jumped and frolicked around the fenced-in pasture, kicking up his legs and doing stallion stuff, showing off to the mares fenced in nearby.

I was mesmerized.

On a sudden impulse, he was mine. I decided I had to have this spirited animal.

We purchased three horses for the farm that day, but The Gray was special. He was my kindred spirit.

Some months later, a New York race horse trainer who had heard about our farm called to take a look at our boarding facilities. He wanted to board race horses during the off season. We set a date.

He arrived at the farm on a Saturday morning, looked at the barn and the boarding facilities. Then he spotted The Gray. His eyes lit up and he said, "I know I can make a Derby winner out of this one."

And so, The Gray went to Belmont. After several months of training he turned out to be fast, responsive and quickly proved the trainer to be right. He had that instinctive, thoroughbred competitive spirit. Most important, he had the the speed and desire to stay ahead of other horses on the track.

The Gray was ready. We began to enter him in races.

We were in the winner's circle several times. It was a thrill, a rush, to see him win, hearing the crowd cheer him on, and watch him strive to beat the other horses. He was a competitive athlete.

Then, that fateful race.

He broke out of the gate and worked his way to the lead.

Nancy Hungerford
Riverton, CT

His ears were up and he was running at a steady gallop.

Suddenly it went wrong. We watched him slow down at the first turn. In spite of a buckled front leg he was still determined, running and trying his best to win.

Skillfully the jockey, in tune with The Gray's movements, brought him to a halt and gently road him off the track, out of the race.

We rushed to the paddock. The trainer said he'd never race again but he would recover given time.

We had sold our Connecticut farm; however, I was assured a farm would be found for him where he could heal. While he would no longer be a race horse, he could become someone's special horse as he had been mine.

I wasn't very savvy about horse racing. It wasn't until I asked for the location of the farm he was sent to that I was gently told what happened to him.

The rude reality of the racing business was explained to me. He had become useless, was lame and was "put down." The trainer had decided it was better not to tell me. He said he wasn't sure I could handle it.

At first I was stunned . . . almost numb. Then my emotions ran from a slow build up of anger to rage. After that came the tears. The words "put down" haunt me to this day.

I never raced another one of our horses nor spoke to the trainer again.

I still enjoy watching the Triple Crown and root for the horse, or horses, I think have "heart."

I listen to the trainers when they are interviewed and take note of the dedicated ones, the ones who have feeling and concern for their charge.

I never worry about a jockey being injured. They have chosen their profession and know the risks involved. I have the greatest admiration for those light weight, strong, skilled athletes. Especially the ones who bond with the horse they are riding and, while striving for a win, attempt to guide them safely around the track.

Nancy Hungerford
Riverton, CT

Yet, the true athlete in the race is the sleek, fast thoroughbred. However, he has nothing to say about his "occupation." It is his owner who has chosen his career for him. His owner is his caretaker and the decisions made for this athlete, as we know, can be thrilling, financially rewarding, yet sometimes heartbreaking.

When I think about the magnificent animal entrusted to me, I simply call him "The Gray."

I have erased his registered name from my mind to help assuage my guilt. It is too painful to admit how ignorant I was and what I could or should have done.

He was in my care, ran for me, won races, displayed his heart and spirit. He didn't deserve to be put down just because he was broken.

It was I who failed The Gray.

Naya Blue
Troy, ME

Women Like Coffee

"I didn't even think they made these any more," he said, pouring water into the new, chrome-percolator coffee pot. She looked up over the newspaper, waiting.

"You know," his voice dipped into what she would hear as a jab, "Starbucks says these things make the worst coffee." Steve's black eyebrows cocked in her direction, anticipating her retort. He knew she would hear what ever he said as an invitation to argue. Jen exhaled behind the paper, Hollywood loud in her exasperation, not wanting to take the bait, which he had carefully cast. She was unable to resist him. As she snapped open her full lips, her eyes hardened.

"I'm not sure what it is you want from me." Her words poked at him edgy and jagged. Steve thought he could hear little chips of glass clinking off her teeth.

"That is the third coffee pot I've brought home in the last six months."

When Jen moved in two years ago, there was an old hand-me-down coffee pot from his aunt. It was a well-used "Coffee-mate," whose plastic had yellowed to the color of his old aunt's teeth. It matched the worn loveseat and turquoise chairs; all flower patterned, circa late 1970's. When they were dating she had mistakenly thought his taste in house wares and furniture had some sense of retro style. She later discovered that each piece had been tenderly dusted off and brought from family attics, by well meaning female relatives after his divorce. Quite unconsciously, he measured her offerings against them. Nothing she could present to him would ever be as trustworthy as the decades old elbow spots, his grandfather rubbed into the hard wood veneer of the kitchen table.

"First, you didn't like the glass pot, it was too old, didn't keep the coffee hot enough. So, I went out and found you a

Naya Blue
Troy, ME

new carafe. That wasn't good enough. Then you wanted an insulated one..." She spat the words through clenched teeth.

His shoulders sank and his ears turned pink. They were learning how to fight with each other. Testing the range and the connection between them. Steve turned to face her, his large hands encompassing his thin hips.

"You aren't listening to me. That's not what I said. I didn't say that 'I' didn't like the coffee pot!" His voice pitched higher, his frustration palpable. "I said, STARBUCKS said it doesn't make good coffee!"

His blue eyes glared at her over his wire-rimmed glasses. Jen enjoyed his annoyance. She knew she shouldn't, but something about his angry resolve drew her closer when they argued.

"Actually, I like perked coffee!" he entreated, eyes on her, waiting.

Relenting, Jen smiled gently, as her hand brushed blonde hair across her forehead. A sign of capitulation, he accepted it tentatively, the same way he accepted her.

Steve turned and as he poured the steaming coffee from the percolator; she realized it looked strikingly like the pot her own grandmother had owned.

D. R. von Hallett
Brunswick, ME

Transatlantic Call

I have pitched my tent
By the river of your voice.
Let the herons come

Vowels distend
slip past us
While consonants
softly wash a stone

How I wait
for the rapids
to snare a rock,
fish that will jump
catching sunlight
on a scale or a fin

But no
your rhythm is slow
so slow ...

Mostly you slug
along flat land
never looking
for a hill
Accepting leaves
or sunlight
to display
as you will
Waiting for me
to plunge
my fist in
pull out one
or the other
for my very own

Jessica Furino
Scotch Pines, NJ

Carlton

Carlton is a middle aged black man who has schizophrenia and is homeless. He lives in a beautiful suburban community. Many of my friends and I have known him for over twenty years. He refuses to take his medication and will not live with his family. He sleeps in the woods and rests in our parks. He is fed and taken care of by the local business people and our community. Our community brings him food and clothing. He rides his bike and collects items that he needs. I don't know how he is able to survive, but he does.

One day, a friend of mine was on his way to make a deposit at the bank. He stopped at the local Quick Check to purchase a cup of coffee. Joe, accidentally, dropped his deposit of three hundred dollars on the ground. As he started up his car, Carlton knocked on his window. Joe was startled. Carlton said, "Excuse me, you dropped this in the store," and proceeded to hand Joe his three hundred dollars.

My friend was overwhelmed by his honesty. He told me that if he were in Carlton's predicament, he wasn't sure he would have done the same thing. Carlton changed my friend, that night. God has truly blessed Carlton.

Lawrence Cann
Winter Haven, FL

Memories of Jack

When I was 4 ½, Grandpa and Grandma moved into half of our house. They had a kitchen and living room downstairs and two bedrooms upstairs. I remember Grandpa and Grandma arriving because on one occasion I was in the woodshed, on the second floor, standing in the open doorway watching them arrive. Nancy was pulling the cart with a hay rack on it loaded with furniture and things. There were three cows tied to the back which would have had a rough trip because the horse moved faster and also the cows were walking on a dirt and stony road. I would imagine that their feet were sore as it was at least four miles between the farms. I believe he brought over eight cows as that was the number that we always had.

The highlight at that time was their dog Jack, who moved in with them. Jack was an English Bulldog that arrived at their door in Pembroke Point one day. Jack was like a wonder dog, full of surprises and always by our side. He is the dog of my childhood. He followed us everywhere. Of course Jack had the usual bag of tricks, such as dead dog, roll over, sit up, lay down, speak and shake hands.

When Grandpa went out in the field to work, Jack went with him. Around 10 AM Grandpa would send Jack back to the house. Jack would go to Grandma's door and bark. She was ready for him and would give Jack a small wicker basket with a firm handle. In the basket was a small jar of milk, a sandwich and a few homemade cookies; all of this was covered with a white napkin. Jack would take the handle in his mouth and head back to Grandpa. Once there, Grandpa stopped whatever he was doing and took the basket to wherever he would be comfortable, on the ground or on a nearby rock. Jack laid down in front of him and watched very closely as the last cookie was for him. The napkin and jar was put

Lawrence Cann
Winter Haven, FL

back in the basket and Jack would return to the house with it. When the deed was completed Jack would return to the field to be with Grandpa.

About a quarter of a mile from our house was a small country store on the corner of Chegoggin Road and Tinpot Road. When Grandpa ran out of Zig Zag cigarette tobacco (20 cents) or cigarette papers (5 cents), he would tie a piece of paper to Jack's collar with the money in it and send Jack to the store.

Jack was no dummy, as our local butcher lived between us and the store which were all on the same side of the road. Jack of course went to the store through the fields and checked out the butcher's area for bones that may have been thrown out for the animals.

At the store, Jack would bark to get Mack's attention. Mack checked the note and then put what was needed in a paper bag. As soon as Jack had the paper bag, he was out the door and off to the field to find Grandpa.

Jack always carried out his mission but after giving Grandpa the bag, he usually disappeared and could later be found knawing on a good size bone. A picture of contentment.

Ronne Gleason
Chesterfield, MI

The Country Choir

Ousting with savor this country air;
Simply wondrous the environ calm
That rushes to my brain a numbing stare.

Chirps from animal life, clear and concise,
So much so, a symphony cannot compete
With melodies so foreign to city entice.

Through the lattice a rare type guest
Meets my eye; a comely deer
It 'tis that lay so unrepressed.

The rustle of weeds, when meeting winds caress,
Chastens the day with tunes that rest
For days and more earth-minded distress.

Glancing into the forest prow,
Wonderment breeds untimely thoughts
Of nature's might and free endow.

Uttering but whispers for your friend to call,
Replies begot so quickly, it seems
The country-like vista has built-in walls.

The sound of quiet, its heavy-laden choir,
Taps a zeal for knowing the caste
Of my lady chosen virgin squire.

Frolic and care, best left anon,
So to compare my childhood play
With a country life I now dwell upon.

Ronne Gleason
Chesterfield, MI

Early to rise, no reason to sleep,
Especially when the sun's great might
Sends its beam upon my sheet.

Surrounding neighbors to church they go
With hopes to live and hopes to die,
'Tis all I can say of them I know.

The rampant gorge of frail pursuits,
Exhausting energy to stem city strife,
Is brought to light by country recruits.

Looking headlong to blue-laden skies,
I viewed the glide of free-reined birds
That durst defies any sorrow to rise.

Aflight from Care to splendors wreaked
From Nature's tunes of timeless tides,
I bathed in waves that purely speak-ed.

G. A. Scheinoha
Eden, WI

Stateside

He always dreamed he'd disappear behind the Iron Curtain, vanish inside Czechoslovakia as if the Bohmerwald had opened up to swallow him. A fact his friend, the gas station jockey warned solemnly of and he scoffed, though secretly wished for.

Not completely. Or forever. Just say, six months. Then he'd reappear, the foreign correspondent who lives to tell the tale. His trenchcoat immaculate as ever, brogans polished to a shimmer, a looking glass glint even Alice could find her way out of.

Or he'd be wearing those heavy, black hiking shoes, low tops with cleats clogged with the good earth gathered up from his roamings round the Slavic countryside, ever the roving reporter. A freelance covering any whim, every inch on foot and by the portable typewriter slung under one arm, the other thrust into his pocket, clutching a press card, his passport, ticket and tool for dredging stories abroad.

He'd be marrow weary, journalism oozed out of each pore till he could bleed no more words. No gulag would hold him, larger than any life or cliche.

Not the hard squint of border guards as their thick accents drizzled like maple syrup around his ears, wrapping him in an onion of suspicion, peeled back to, "What is your business in Praha?"

To drink, he thinks to say, wondering if perhaps they'll catch the significance, if journalists are indeed the same the world over, in search of a story and a beverage, not necessarily in that order. He suppresses a smile. He's sure these guards wouldn't understand.

Nor can he state he's to meet Vaclav Havel, the dissident who's more a torch up the Czech Comms' butt in a cellar bar somewhere. Perhaps share a litre of white wine, dry as

G. A. Scheinoha
Eden, WI

Havel's voice falling, dense as smoke from his cigarettes, gaze piercing through the haze to pin the corresponded to whatever truth lies between them.

And then reality washes over him with sobering waves of not what might have been but always is. He's never been overseas, much less to Prague.

UPI doesn't call, Reuters has never heard of him. And now, The Wall's gone. The dissident became president, then retired from public life, even further distant from an actual meeting with this newsman wannabe.

He's just a hack, correspondent all right, along with a thousand other so-called freelancers; janitors, bartenders, dishwashers by day, outliving and lasting the menial at night, when they cast for the lure, bait that unknown, faceless fish named editor for a third-string wire service will swallow. Yanking them across the other to fulltime footing, respect as a writer.

Sounding him off into deep, dangerous but welcome waters. "Careful what you wish for," he whispers to the darkness, a mantra of fulfillment.

Still...the dreamer is no bigger than the scope of his dreams. Or fictions he unfolds afterwards, carefully creased remembrances of the one that got away.

David Campbell
Cape Elizabeth, ME

The Living and the Dead

for Patsea

Two preachers spelled each other
reading out below the crow's nest pulpit
their approval of ninety years that went
preparing to meet her God.
All sobs shut down at their source.
O death, I wondered, where is thy sting?
O life, how precisely was it
"she left the world a better place?"
More crowded, yes: King's Chapel
overflowed with kinfolk in the wake
of your childless great aunt Almy.

The first-rate organ gave a Bach Prelude.
We had our daughters close
in cozy breakfast-nook pews.
Anglican captives, we stood as told,
sat ramrod, stood and hymned the numbers,
sat. I watched the milky window light
cut the spring midday to churchly dusk
on plain beige walls, a thin extract
where still the personal hung fire
and called for more, for story,
for colors deep-staining
through complex family filigree.

David Campbell
Cape Elizabeth, ME

Only the serving crew was hushed
in the old-wealth time-capsule club
where the tribe gossiped reunion:
boardroom males, hearty as beefsteak;
ladies like dry salt reeds
rustling the air, lined up to be,
each one, the Last of Her Line.

"I'll look like that when I get old,"
you said as we left the reception.
And I will too, my consort, compeer,
true companion—I a fluff-headed reed
of the Yankee tideland,
where another migrated southerner,
magnolia, roots in the Back Bay fill
and waits out one more freezing Boston April.

Short legs sized up Commonwealth Avenue
and whined. You scaled down the mission:
"See those trees? That's where we're going."
They went, already seeing full-feathered
the swan boat that likely would not be there,
the bronze mother duck and ducklings that would.
"We'll cross you," we said,
and held tight and flowed over curbs
like spidery tandem vehicles.

Between the lone wolf trail
and the bonded circlings of the pack
I walked into an image of my own,
became a branch on your family tree
between the living and the dead,
new growth at my bare twig ends
in soft camelia-petal hands.

Kathy Ott McHugh
Dover, NH

My Two Grandmothers

Both of my grandmothers were born in the late 1890's and lived throughout the era of Virginia Woolf, when women were limited as persons in numerous ways; the accepted practice of the time. Yet those who had the privilege of knowing or being raised by these women benefited from their expertise, personal strength and knowledge. They may have been held back by the status quo etched in stone, yet they were known to speak or demonstrate their strong opinions whenever put to the test.

My grandmothers worked hard; farming, cooking, canning, sewing, washing and cleaning at a time when there were no microwaves, washing machines, refrigerators or sufficient indoor plumbing. They ironed clothes and linens before the days of permanent press. In addition to family duties, one worked in a silk mill and the other was the caretaker of church linens. Before the introduction of modern appliances, little energy was left for holding public office or running for the school board, roles that women are more accepted in today.

Nevertheless, my grandmothers made known exactly what they stood for in the issues and concerns of their day, like prohibition. Fearing it was known about in the neighborhood, my maternal grandmother poured down the drain the "hooch" my grandfather created, to his chagrin. My paternal grandmother was frugal with whatever she had, due to her years of poverty as a single parent of four children, as well as surviving the Great Depression. No wonder why her favorite expression even years later was "Waste not, want not."

Although they lived five hundred miles apart, my grandmothers had similar stories. Neither of them drove a car and rarely went to town, yet they read a lot and became quite adept at giving good advice and imparting knowledge to those

Kathy Ott McHugh
Dover, NH

who were willing to spend time with them and listen. Both of my grandmothers had four children—two sons and two daughters. Both became Gold Star Mothers. Each lost a son in World War II, one in a bomber plane crash in Florida, the other in the march to St. Lo following the invasion of Normandy, France. I can only imagine the excruciating sorrow they felt when a military officer appeared at each of their doors, bearing the sad news of their sons' passing. There were memorial services and dedications for their sons in their towns. Years later each mother still regretted not saying goodbye or giving their sons an extra hug the morning they left home for the service of their country.

Neither of my grandmothers had ideal childhoods, lives or marriages. Times were tough in the years 1920-1940. Without their obvious personal strength, their families would have had difficulty surviving. Had these women not been confined or constricted by family responsibilities left to them by husbands who were not dependable along with the rules society placed women under, they would have made a huge difference in politics or business, as they were obvious pillars of strength and conviction.

My paternal grandmother and her family owned and operated a co-op cheese factory. This endeavor required much diverse knowledge of cheese making, running machines and storing the product as well as compensating the farmers, tracking income and supplies. My grandmother's father died on Armistice Day in 1918, so the rest of the immediate family took over the cheese factory. When Gram's brother died of diphtheria, the business was sold; replaced with a small home on seven acres of farmland. My paternal grandmother got married in 1921, and they purchased a small inn and a lumber saw mill, all of which was destroyed by fire in 1926. Gram and her three children moved in with Gram's mother who had lost all of her savings between the fire, bankruptcy and loaning family money. She worked as a mid-wife. Gram's husband filed for bankruptcy, then took

Kathy Ott McHugh
Dover, NH

the only work he could find which was far from home. After they had one more child, he was rarely seen again. However, this gram and her children came through these hard times, primarily due to her being the person of admirable strength and frugal determination she was. She never ran from or shirked her responsibilities; that's for certain.

My maternal grandmother was an only child, born in Vermont in 1895. After her parents divorced, she and her mother relocated to the industrial city of Manchester, New Hampshire to live with relatives. My grandparents were married in 1917, but my grandfather had to leave to serve his country in World War I. They spent sixty-five years together. My grandfather thrived on sports, alcohol, fishing, friends and popularity at the clubs even when they were raising their four children. Without complaint, Gram sat home many a day and night while Gramp was out, content with her crossword puzzles and mystery books, sitting in her favorite chair near the window sill filled with violets.

Gram was a great seamstress, who made most of the family clothing. She made delicious homemade pies and did a lot of canning, as they had a big garden. She loved watching musicals on Saturday and Sunday nights, as well as comedy shows. She used expressions such as "Ayuh" and "Oh Fiddlesticks!"

Both of my grandmothers lived well into their eighties. Virginia Woolf and my two grandmothers had so much to offer and made their mark in their own ways, as women of their time could only be repressed for so long. These ladies may not have had the opportunity to attend college, yet they read a lot and kept up with the news and knew exactly what was going on. Although women of their time were often referred to as the weaker sex, these women were the actual worthy leaders who gave their families their best and true direction; the independently educated viewpoint that was needed at the time of economic upheaval. These women kept the coal burning in the stoves, passing on the irons to their

Kathy Ott McHugh
Dover, NH

daughters, granddaughters and great granddaughters like me and you who carry on the tradition of making a difference as women. It is we who are their hope.

My grandmothers both lost relatives to depression and suicide. Each life was a worthy and valuable one, never to be forgotten. Maybe Virginia Woolf was personally haunted before and during that day by depression or the sexual abuse she experienced by her two half-brothers. Nevertheless, female writers lost a true role model the day Virginia walked out into the water weighed down by the rocks in her pockets. Let us continue to carry on the great legacy Virginia began with her written work, renewing our commitments to our firmly contributing purpose for all who came before us as well as those who will follow...

Maude Olsen
South Bristol, ME

Power Out

We sit here in the dark and listen;
    A tree blew down somewhere
The wind is whipping up again.
The cedar is dancing and the wind whips around the door.
We sit in the dark and listen.
    A tree blew down somewhere.

Without the lights the heavens really show off.
    Every star shines bright and steady.
    Get out the chart, you can follow it to a T.
What man misses by lighting up his streets and houses!
    The brilliant beauty of the starlit sky.
It is quiet now except for the wind and the steady hum
    of the gas heater.
We sit in the dark and wait.
    Somewhere a tree blew down.

***

Show-Off

The Sun went down in glory
Right before my eyes:
Gray clouds above were dusted pink;
The river ran deep blue,
And light streamed out between the trees
In a game of Peek-a-boo.
With streaks of gold and spots of red,
Old Sol prepared to go to bed.

I'd never seen such showmanship
And I stood mesmerized!

Gregg Mosson
Baltimore, MD

Harmony of Apples

One winter I compiled
        from a dim library—
composed of evenings
        stolen from work and sunsets—
                a strange new poem

and then plowed home
        through deep snowdrifts
with my words in a loose-leaf
        solely to be offered
                to you as a present,

and though you took it.
        and though I let you,
something faltered, grew cold and awkward—
        our grievance river disturbed, grew rough, louder-
                a drawbridging of hearts.

Then one autumn
        as I arrived from the orchard
with a basket of apples
        and sprigs in my hair,
                and a pocketful of notes

for a new long poem,
        and stood on the threshold—
I spilled my apples there.
        They ran across the floor,
                and sort of like bobbing

Gregg Mosson
Baltimore, MD

but with the sound of knocking,
    we scrambled together
to gather the apples
    stealing the kitchen
        and turning it to summer.

The small pages
    jotted with letters
written in a hand
    shattered by expression
        burst in the air.

and like a gust of winter
    that swoops into a den
of old, quiet lovers
    who have opened the flue
        to let out the burning.

we sat on the floor
    ordering our possessions
and playing with apples.
    Our hands bridged across
        what years had cost.

Darling, you remain the only
    one I want
        to speak to about my life.

Roslyn Morrill
Rockport, ME

Past Perfect

One continuous view
especially in winter,
of sea and land and trees.
Intersprinkled with houses,
well ordered.
Take a handful of marbles,
see where they land.
A better result.
Road signs obliterate suspense.
All discovered, labeled, exploited.
No surprises.
“You CAN get there from here!”
to anywhere that you couldn't before.
Nostalgia, longing for what isn’t.
Remaining unchanged would have been progress.

***

Janice Marcopulos
Rockport, ME

Dolphin

Splashy, playful cunning
As he dives again, nose first
Swimming wherever the current goes,
Sometimes pushing against it
Taking deep breaths of salt air
As his friends can't keep up,
his acquaintances fall back.
Now he is really alone.

James A. Southern
Shepherdsville, KY

Fishing Battle

Spring, a time of renewal. The long cold months of winter are now past and the warmth of this spring morning is welcomed. Today was going to be just like a thousand other mornings when my father and I would go fishing. We would wake before dawn, fry eggs for sandwiches, brew coffee for our thermos, and check our equipment. After purchasing gas for the truck and bait for the fish, we would be on our way. Today was going to be different.

This day was going to be different from all the thousand other fishing trips because I had a plan. My father sat in the driver's seat staring out at the road, but not really looking at it. I could tell he was imagining the day's events and how they would unfold. His preoccupation was evident by the slight smile on his face. Just like a thousand other times. He knew once we arrived and had gotten set-up, he would catch the most fish. I never could figure out whether he enjoyed catching so many fish, or if his delight came from rubbing it in. After he realized he had a comfortable lead in numbers he would begin to taunt me. "I smell a skunk," he would say with a broad smile on his face. All I could do was return his smile with a smirk on my face and reply, "I'm right behind you." I never caught up. Today was going to be different.

As my father drove, he lit a cigarette and inhaled deeply. Totally at peace with his surroundings and comfortable in the knowledge of the outcomes of the day, he was completely oblivious of my devious plans. Over the last several months, I had spent every free moment reading fishing magazines and watching fishing shows. I felt the vast knowledge I had acquired now prepared me to do battle with my father. This time, I was going to win. This time I would taunt him and he would see me as an equal, not the forever student. With my new found knowledge I scoured the fishing supply

James A. Southern
Shepherdsville, KY

stores until I gathered an assortment of gear that would rival the great Bill Dance himself. I was absolutely confident victory was going to be mine.

As we crested the last hill, Norris Lake loomed before us. It was beautiful, as the morning sun shown fully on the open water, burning off the last of the mist. The water moved in a silent dance reflecting the light, bouncing it in every direction. My dad slowed the pick-up to ten miles-per-hour. The paved road had turned to dirt and there were several pot holes. As we bounced along, Dad's eyes fixed on the lake. "It's going to be a great day!" he shouted over the roar of the engine, as we ground to a halt several feet from the water's edge.

Exiting the vehicle, we began to assemble our gear. Dad always fished with two complete tackle boxes, which held over two hundred items in each. In addition he had three fishing rods, a thermos and a bag with sandwiches. There he stood, tall and proud with all his equipment perfectly in position, ready to go into action. "Are you ready?" I could hear the anticipation in his voice.

"Yeah," I replied. *In more ways than one,* I thought to myself as I grabbed the last of my things from the truck.

Arriving at the water's edge we began to assemble our fishing rods and open our tackle boxes. I positioned myself a few yards away from my dad so I could work my magic without his seeing. I started by tying a new spinner bait on the end of my line.

Of all the articles I had read, this particular bait was recommended by all the top fishermen. Its body was an iridescent green with a black head and white eyes. In front of the bait was a polished silver plate called a "spoon" that moved back-and-forth as you cranked it through the water. According to the experts, it would drive the fish wild. After a few tries I felt that familiar tug. I had a fish! Without arousing too much commotion, I brought my prize into the bank. It was a nice bass, about 12 inches long. Good enough to keep. I silently placed the fish on a stringer and lowered him into the water. My plan was simple. I would catch as many fish as I could and when my father caught a few and started to brag, I would show him my catch.

As I began to cast again, I leaned to my right to observe my father. He was sitting in the same place and it appeared that he had not moved. He'd lit another cigarette and the smoke slowly lifted from his motionless form. He seemed to be staring out over the water as if some strange mythical being had him mesmerized. After a few more casts, bam! I had another. The second fish was a real beauty. It was about a two pound walleye and in my excitement I almost called out to my father. Then I remembered the plan. I quietly placed the second fish on the stringer and both fish began to fight with each other in an attempt to gain their freedom. I placed them in the water and turned to observe my father. He sat in the same position, his cigarette burned away and he was still staring out over the water.

I almost went over to check on him but decided against it. I renewed my efforts on fishing with the intention of making my plan a success. Everything was going great.

I had two fish and my father had nothing. Today was going to be the greatest day of my life. The sun now shown in all its glory and it was a beautiful morning, the air was crisp and clean. There were no traffic noises, no boats cruising the lake, only me, Dad and the fish. As I sat daydreaming, a third fish decided to give my bait a try. We fought for a few minutes before I hauled him in. It was a gorgeous catfish, about 2 ½ - 3 pounds. He pulled from side-to-side attempting to snap the line. I reeled him in and grabbed at his bottom lip, bringing my prize to me.

After getting the catfish on the stringer, I thought, *Now is the time to rub it in on old Dad.* I grabbed my stringer from the water and hoisted it high above my head. The fish in utter terror began to thrash against each other, spraying me with water. With an enormous smile on my face I turned to my

James A. Southern
Shepherdsville, KY

father. "I have the first three fish," I shouted.

To my bewilderment my father was not sitting where I had last seen him. Instead he had moved from his position and was now standing knee deep in the lake. Using both hands, he was holding the biggest catfish I'd ever seen. This monster later weighed in at 27 pounds. "I'll bet your three don't weigh as much as my one!" he shouted back. Completely amazed I dropped my three fish on the bank. They began to flop and roll in a vain effort to get back in the water. Coming to my senses, I reached down, unsnapped the stringer, and let them go.

I moved over to help my father get his fish on a stringer. Angry at being caught, the giant catfish whipped her tail around as if she was trying to swat us away. Dad looked at me as if to say, "Isn't she a beauty." The smile on his face was as proud as I've ever seen him.

This made my defeat even bitterer. Today was going to be my day. *What had happened?* I read all the magazines, watched all the shows, and felt as though I had all the knowledge needed to be the victor. What I had not calculated into my equation was one simple element that my dad had utilized, instinct. He knew the climate, he knew the terrain, he knew the water temperature and he knew what it would take to catch the fish that he caught. I bowed my head in defeat. But it was not as bitter as you might think. I got my revenge on that fish. She was served up with some fried potatoes, corn bread and beans. It was a wonderful meal, thanks to my dad.

My dad has been gone for eight years now. When time permits I go to that same spot on the bank of Norris Lake, I sit down and bait a line, and in the cool dampness of the early morning I think of him and smile.

GOOSE RIVER ANTHOLOGY, 2011

We seek selections of fine poetry, essays, and short stories (3,000 words or less) for the 9th annual *Goose River Anthology, 2011.* Book will be beautifully produced with full color cover and hard covers will have a full color dust jacket.

You may submit even if you have been published before in a previous edtion of the *GRA.* We retain one-time publishing rights. All rights revert back to the author after publication. You may submit as many pieces as you like.

EARN CASH ROYALTIES. Author will receive a 10% royalty on all sales that he or she generates.

There is no purchase required and nothing is required of the author for publication. Deadline for submissions is March 31, 2011. Publication will be Fall, 2011 (in time for Christmas gifts). Guidelines are as follows:

- Submit clean-typed copy and if possible **(not required)** an electronic copy of the work either in Word or Word Perfect. File can be submitted on a floppy, CD or e mailed (e mail preferred).
- Reading fee: $1.00 per page
- Do not put two poems on the same page
- Essays and short stories should be double-spaced
- SASE for notification (.44 cents) plus additional postage for possible return of submission if desired
- Author's name & address at top of each page

Submit to:
Goose River Anthology, 2011
3400 Friendship Road
Waldoboro, ME 04572-6337
Telephone: (207) 832-6665
E mail: gooseriverpress@roadrunner.com
www.gooseriverpress.com

www.ingramcontent.com/pod-product-compliance
Lightning Source LLC
Chambersburg PA
CBHW020548310726
48979CB00008B/1141/J

* 9 7 8 1 5 9 7 1 3 1 0 0 1 *